THE PRAIRIE FIGHTER

A thousand miles beyond civilisation lay an empire second to none in the raw, wild world of the Far West. Here came men of every creed and principle, and men without either principles or creeds, to battle for the wealth of this savage world. Jud Parker was one of that enduring, fierce breed. He needed no gun to blast his way to wealth and power, but only the time necessary to mould lesser men to his desires. Jud Parker's kind survived the hell-roaring days to found financial dynasties. They clawed their way to the top ruthlessly and looked down from their heights on lesser mortals.

THE PRAIRIE FIGHTER

Claude Cassady

A Lythway Book

CHIVERS PRESS
BATH

First published in Great Britain 1963
by
Robert Hale Limited
This Large Print edition published by
Chivers Press
by arrangement with Robert Hale Limited
1983

ISBN 0 85046 938 4

British Library Cataloguing in Publication Data

Cassady, Claude
  The prairie fighter.—Large print ed.—
  (A Lythway book)
  Rn: Lauran Payne   I. Title
  813'.54 [F]   PS3566.A34

  ISBN 0–85046–938–4

THE PRAIRIE FIGHTER

CHAPTER ONE

The Dakotas lay in the middle distance, not only in space but also in time. Northward were immense plains and thrusting saw-toothed mountains that did not end until the whiteness of Canada terminated against that great greyness which was the Far North. Southward was the outfall of a huge landmass which climbed the Continental Divide, then plunged onward relentlessly for hundreds and thousands of miles until an ocean abruptly stopped it. Eastward beyond the Plains of Laramie, the Plains of Kansas, the Plains of Nebraska, lay a variety of civilisation, a kind of culture, a kind of lawful orderliness which the Dakotas lacked. Westward, across interminable north-south mountain ranges, was an unwanted land where gold could be found, and good land, and the kind of seclusion the men who braved this fierce country often sought and usually needed— safety from legal processes.

Everything west of the Missouri, north of the Divide, east of Vancouver's Island and south of the Canadian line acknowledged the Dakotas as the heartland of this middle-distance frontier empire.

Men rode and limped and clawed their way to towns such as Fargo, Deadwood, Fort Berthold,

Bismarck, Grand Forks, Rapid City and Sioux City. They paralleled the Missouri River, they crossed and recrossed it. They bull-boated its serpentine treacherous north-to-east curving bringing with them for sale, for trade, for hell-raising all the gleanings of a year and sometimes longer in the gold-hills or along the beaver creeks. They came with almost breathless expectation; with prodigious thirsts and lusts. They came armed and soiled and bearded, defiant, challenging, uncontrollably exuberant. But they invariably brought with them the *parfleches* of smoke-tanned buckskin swelling with gold, the bales of prime plews, the solid substance in all its variety which made the Dakotas prosperous and kept them booming.

A different breed of men came out of the eastern distances to this teeming, sprawling, struggling world; men, usually better clothed, better read and spoken, who, when placed in one of the seething towns, seemed not to fit by reason of attire, erudition, paleness of face and softness of hands.

But one had only to look into their eyes, to consider the set of their lips, to recognise that an identical ferocity existed. As a matter of fact these were the most thoroughly lawless men of them all, and their purpose was not to grub out the gold nor lay and tend trap lines, nor weigh out the flour and set the ox shoes; their purpose in being in the Dakotas was to achieve wealth, to forge power, to establish domination if they could, to pit themselves tooth and fang against any and all. They were different from the buckskin buccaneers. They avoided working with their hands. They rarely carried guns— sometimes did not even own guns. Yet as economic pioneers they could and would acquire a stranglehold on this middle-empire's financial life-blood and when the uninhibited colourful childish, booted spurred two-gun simpleton with his broad-brimmed big hat, his checkered red shirt and his squandered life was finally swept away, these latter-day genuine robber barons would continue to scheme and brawl and claw over one another's empires—and bodies.

Big Jud Parker was one of these prairie pirates. He stood well over six feet tall in his naked feet and stripped down and wringing wet he weighed half as much as a grassed-out short yearling beef—or nearly so anyway. His face was handsome in a way that men could appreciate, but it entirely lacked the kind of sly gentleness women liked. The eyes were dark blue and bold-staring. The nose, twice broken, had flaring nostrils and a hawkish arch. The mouth was wide, a little thin at lip-line, and masculinely wilful. Jud Parker's jaw, though, was the key to his entire personality and character; it was heavy, square and massive: the jaw of a fighter. His head rode easily upon a columnar neck and below it was a breadth of chest and shoulder no man was ever born with— he had to acquire it through gruelling physical labour.

Jud had worked in the Pennsylvania mines; he had felled timber and goaded oxen. He had brawled his way across half a continent before he'd awakened to the fact that only fools and drunks work with their muscles. After that, in the best clothing money could buy, a tall silk hat and an Ascot tie of purest silk, he'd made the overland crossing to Dakota, a titan of a man who, after recklessly spending his early years, was now resolved to conquer in a different fashion. A genuine prairie pirate.

He strode the teeming byways of Seward City with the air of a man who could command all that he saw. Summer dust jerked to life under his boots and the rough men of this rough land, some in buckskin, some in butternut and some in ragged woollens, moved clear for him to pace past. He looked the dude with his silk hat and once-white shirt, with his Ascot and the flashing stickpin that was shaped like a horseshoe set with diamonds. But the men of this land—with their lives depending upon inherent ability to judge other men—saw beyond these things; saw the thick-thewed thighs, the easy-rolling shoulders and bull-bass chest. They gave way before Jud Parker's thrusting stride; they looked after him; they saw and appraised and

4

evaluated. Instinct told them solemnly this rock-hard big man with the challenging eyes had not in his makeup one ounce of fear or doubt or compassion. He might make a good friend, occasionally men like Jud Parker did make a good friend, but of a lethal certainty they always and invariably made a good enemy. They were in this respect like an Indian; they might forgive but they never forgot.

Jud was fresh from the stage. He'd found a room—dingy and redolent of carelessly tended chamber pots—for ten dollars a week, which was a fortune to him at this time. He'd left his carpet-bag there and was bound now for the Warbonnet Saloon, a log-and-mud-wattle square building on Seward City's main thoroughfare—Front Street.

He took the Warbonnet by storm, as he'd always done upon entering any room because physically he'd never seemed built for being indoors. He dwarfed other men and made even the chairs and tables seem fragile. Where men stood at the bar nearly shoulder to shoulder he thrust his way in turning his smile, which was half challenging, half questioning, upon those who looked around in disapproval at this powerful jostling.

'Sour mash,' he called to the harassed barman, and struck the bar with a scarred big fist. His drink came at once. He threw it off neat and put down the glass, turned and leaned

5

there, big arms hooked upon the bar on either side of him. There were men east of the wide Missouri who could have accurately described big Jud Parker's thoughts at this moment; with liquor alive and moving in him, with his wide-planted legs and bent-back arms. With those great bony fists hanging there. Jud was savouring a good moment; he was inwardly exulting over finding this new land so entirely to his liking, and he was gazing almost fondly upon the shifting, moving mass of men and girls, seeking something, perhaps someone, upon whom to let loose the full run of his exultation. This day, those knowledgeable people could have correctly prophesied, would end for Jud Parker in a fight, a kiss, or a primeval roar of sheer exuberance.

He faced back around. 'Another one,' he bellowed, spinning the glass away from him. 'A double shot this time.'

As before he downed the drink in one swallow and smiled broadly through a sudden gush of blinked-away tears. 'Green as grass,' he gasped. 'Made last night and aged between midnight and breakfast time. The rottenest whisky I ever drank in my life.'

The barman's face was wholly impassive. He said simply, 'Six bits, mister.'

Jud threw down the coins and turned to again cast his bold stare out over the smoky room.

There were a few harridans moving through

6

the throng of men. Mostly, these were freighters in high-topped cowhide boots with flat heels, or miners with rolled-up flannel sleeves and unkempt beards. There were also a few bucks in antelope breeches, some with fringes, some without, and here and there a townsman with sleeve-garters and maybe a pushed-back derby hat. Least common but still represented were the stockmen, the range-cattlemen with spurs and wide-brimmed low-crowned hats and shell-belted pistols. This saloon was like a river between whose two banks flowed the surging, pausing, hastening, loafing or scheming wash of Dakota Territory humanity. The air was alive with sounds, with smoke, with powerful odours. Men were forever entering and departing. There was a restlessness here that Jud had noticed imbued the entire countryside. Everyone had something to do, some place to go, some means for making money. The whisky was working in him strongly now and his smile lingered. This was the land he'd been seeking all his life. A country as big and raw and brawling as he was. An empire tailored to his private measurements. A land where anything went and where big Jud Parker belonged.

He left the bar shouldering his way past to the roadside doorway oblivious of the quick looks of annoyance from those weathered countenances in his wake; the men he'd unceremoniously jostled aside.

7

Outside the long day's summertime brightness was beginning to fade out a little; to turn from brassy blue to an azure paleness. Dusk was not far off.

Front Street's inordinate breadth—deliberately laid out that way in order to accommodate two freight wagons abreast—was layered under five inches of pure dust. Riders passed, wagons and gigs whirled by, and people angled through this constant traffic hastening from one side to the other. Everyone hastening to reach some private destination.

Both sides of Front Street had buildings, some newer than others, all catering to this floodtide of humanity. There was one bank, three liverybarns, several general stores—called emporiums—a number of cafés, two harness shops that Jud could see from where he stood in front of the Warbonnet Saloon, a land and abstract office, saloons galore, even a dressmaker's shop and a bakery. Front Street ran due north and south. Bisecting it were a number of easterly and westerly byways; along these quieter avenues were residences, some hastily erected of slats and tarpaper, others of planed lumber with handsome coats of good white paint. These latter structures with their baywindows, their curlicues and rising roofs, attested to a variety of prosperity usually associated with the Eastern Seaboard, not with the Far West.

8

They brought forth in big Jud Parker's dark blue stare a glinting hard surge of acquisitiveness. He had never lived in a fine house, had never in fact moved in the society of people who did, but with the liquor alive in him now and with his unshakable confidence in himself in this way additionally buttressed, he fiercely promised himself that he would, one day soon, live in the finest painted house in Seward City. He did not even consider how a person with slightly less than one hundred dollars in the money-belt next to his skin could ever hope to accomplish this. The details of existence had never troubled him in the slightest; he was a man who thought always in a manner of grand conquests—with money, with women, with anything which interested him. He would live in one of those proud houses if he had to lie, to cheat, to steal, even to kill, because this was his goal and he ignored all else in this, as he'd always scorned details in all things.

Maturity can come to a man at any time. To some it never comes; these are the boy-men of this world; they're still playing baseball when other men are founding fortunes. Seldom do two men mature at the same time or in the same way. Jud Parker's own maturing had been long coming, but somewhere between Sioux Falls and Seward City it had blossomed forth into a full blooming. He did not know this himself. He knew only as he stood there in the puddling dusk of early evening that every process of thought, living and breathing, was wholly bent to this new and powerful motivation which now claimed him.

He would live in one of those white-painted houses! He would claw and bite and kick and fight his way to the top of the heap in Seward City! He would do this if it killed him; if it killed others. He would have everything which went with success; money, power, respect, adulation. He would hold in his big scarred hands the destinies of men; he would mould and bend— and break—these hastening frontiersmen around him; these hardy frontier spirits whom he could now, from the eminence of his height in front of the Warbonnet Saloon, look down upon feeling for them an impersonal kind of kinship. Kinship without mercy.

Thus did maturity finally come to Jud Parker while he was in his late twenties and over a thousand miles from the place where he'd been born.

He watched the far-away hills rise up starkly to stand in darkening splendour below the lowering sun, feeling as a lord of hosts would feel gazing serenely out over the tents and stacked arms of his legions. He heeded the diminishing traffic as supper hour approached, and afterwards, with the first faint and yeasty starshine-ferment covering eventide with its pewter hue. He strode along the length of Front

10

Street considering the stores, the wares, the people, as an emperor might have considered them feeling pleased at their prosperity and satisfied with their robustness, for these were the things which would enrichen him.

He was passing a saloon when a man's body, propelled outwards with considerable violence, flung across his way to land asprawl in the darkening roadside dust. Jud stopped, gazed outward and watched the man roll over and get up on all fours to hang there like an animal, except that his head sagged forward. He was, Jud knew from experience, willing to get up, to fight on, but willing only in spirit; the man's body was far beyond obeying its owner's will.

A second man came through the spindle-doors; he was fiercely bearded, attired as a freighter and built like a blacksmith. He made for the downed man without a word, his great arms corded with straining, his ham-like fists curled. Jud watched him catch up the lowered form, hold it one-handed as a terrier holds a rat, then sledge a meaty blow into the belly, strike the limp form again and again.

Then Jud moved.

The big freighter had no warning. Jud's fist caught him solidly under the right ear. Pain from that blow like an electric shock travelled all the way to Jud's shoulder. The freighter dropped the smaller man, tried instinctively to twist away, then his knees buckled and he

11

crashed down face forward into the dirt. He did not move again; dust spurted upwards around him.

Jud rubbed his knuckles; the man's skull had been of iron. He turned slightly as other men came crowding out of the saloon to stand gawking.

'Get a bucket of water,' he commanded, and two men moved swiftly back into the saloon to obey. When they returned Jud said, 'Never mind the lad. Throw it on your freighter-friend. He looks like a man worth working off a little energy on.' He was still rubbing his bruised hand, but also he was smiling.

The freighter came to life sputtering. He sat up, probed under his ear with exploring fingers, then he rolled a stare upon Jud as black as midnight and called Jud a bitter name. The men with the water helped him upright then took their bucket and moved away. Someone over by the saloon was gleefully calling for others inside to hurry out there was going to be a fight. The crowd grew and stirred.

'You better not try it,' Jud said to the big freighter. 'Not now anyway, mister. You're not up to it.'

The freighter mouthed that same bitter name again, but made no move forward. He was assessing big Jud Parker and coming to several simultaneous conclusions. Finally he said, 'Mister; what's your name?'

'Jud Parker. What's your's?'

'Caleb Brownell. Mister; I aim to remember you.'

Jud's flaring nostrils drew back a great lungful of warm evening air. 'Any time,' he said. 'Any time at all, Mister Brownell.'

'You got a gun under them fancy clothes?' Brownell demanded.

'No.'

'A knife?'

Jud held up his fists. 'Only these,' he told the freighter.

'Next time we meet they ain't going to be enough.'

Jud let his arms hang loose. He smiled broadly into Caleb Brownell's face. His eyes flicked over the other man briefly. 'You better go soak your head in a bucket of water,' he said, and turned upon his heel, crossed to where Brownell's earlier victim was struggling to his feet, took the youth's arm and walked him fully across the roadway. Jud was feeling thoroughly happy and fulfilled. He'd never before in his life felt so completely at home.

CHAPTER TWO

The man Jud had rescued was a range-cattle-man; he wore the spurred boots, neckerchief and stiff-brimmed hat of his kind but his hip-holster held no gun. He was lithe and graceful and at first glance seemed no more than a boy, but actually he was the same age as Jud. He had trouble making his way so Jud helped him along with one huge arm. They entered another saloon and as usual Jud forced passage to the bar. There, he called for two drinks then told the rangeman to drink up, that his stomach cramps would depart when the liquor hit down into him. They drank.

'I'll kill him,' gasped the rangeman, feeling his middle. 'I'll go back and kill the. . . .'

'What for?' Jud said, his interest centred upon this new-found companion. 'What was it—a fight?'

'Yes.'

Jud considered. The rangeman was half a head shorter than Brownell had been and he was easily sixty pounds lighter. Jud sighed, gestured, for refills, and shook his head wryly.

'Better not try it with your fists again,' he said. 'Your whiskered friend's got a skull of granite.'

The rangeman's hand fell to his hip-holster.

14

He looked down, found it empty and ripped out a curse. Jud laughed.

'Guns're cheap enough,' he told the rangeman. 'You can get another one. What was it all about?'

'His goddamned wagons are in my meadow. Eleven of 'em. His horses and oxen are trampling down my winter feed.' The rangeman considered his refilled shot glass, then flung back his head and tossed off the greasy liquor. He coughed, ground his teeth and spat aside into the sawdust. 'That's Caldwell's doings.'

Jud looked around, saw a recently vacated table and took the rangeman to it, along with their two glasses and a bottle. When they were seated he said, 'Who is Caldwell—your partner?'

'Partner!' Exclaimed the cowman, then, despite his aches, he smiled at Jud. 'Yeah; he's my partner all right.' He called Caldwell a name. 'Heber Caldwell's your partner as soon as he invests a little money in you. He's the banker hereabouts. He's the richest man in the Black Hills country, mister. He's a vicious, conniving old son of. . . .'

'What's he got to do with Brownell?'

'He's Brownell's backer in the cartage business.' The rangeman poured himself a liberal drink and downed it. Colour returned to his face, he settled deeper into his chair and turned a warm look upon big Jud Parker. 'My

15

name's Buck Loring,' he said in an altered tone of voice. 'What's yours?'

'Jud Parker.'

'Well, Jud, by golly, I'm obliged to you. I didn't see you drop Brownell but I wish I had.'

'That's all right,' said Jud. 'Did you borrow money from this Heber Caldwell?'

'Yes; for stocker cattle. Last fall some Texas drovers arrived here with a herd; they were plumb beat and offered their critters at a steal. I went to old man Caldwell and he loaned me the money. I gave him a mortgage on my holdings. I got four thousand acres of land twenty miles out along the Elk River. 'Used to be Indian land. I needed those damned cattle real bad to get going.'

'How much did you borrow?'

'Five thousand dollars.'

'Well; didn't you pay up on time? Why did Caldwell tell Brownell to camp in your meadow?'

'Sure I pay on time. Once a year, every year. Jud; you don't know Heber Caldwell. When he makes a loan he commences tellin' the feller who borrowed from him how to part his hair. He told Brownell—at least this is what Brownell said to me before the fight started—that he owned more of my Pothook Ranch than I owned, and that Brownell could graze his critters anywhere he pleased on my land.'

Jud thoughtfully poured himself another

16

drink and sipped it. There was an opportunity here, he felt, but for the moment it escaped him. He had dropped Caleb Brownell not because of any pity for the rangeman, really, but because when big Jud Parker had been drinking he fought or made love or roared like a bear. But half drunk or fully sober Jud Parker's acquisitive acuity functioned perfectly. It was functioning that way right now; he wanted to know more about the richest man in Seward City. 'Drink up,' he said to Buck Loring, pushing the bottle forward. 'Besides owning you and Brownell who else does Caldwell own hereabouts?'

Loring regarded the liquor bottle solemnly as though balancing a decision in his mind, then he turned away from it resolutely. 'One more drink,' he said, 'and I'll go out and cull wildcats tonight. Caldwell? He owns most of Seward City one way or another. He's got money out on interest all over the Territory. The miners work for him, the freighters, the cowmen like me, even most of the cussed merchants here in town. Jud; you recollect seein' a big white-painted two-storeyed house west of town settin' back in about thirty acres of trees and grass?'

'I saw some white-painted houses; maybe one of them was like that. What of it?'

'That's old Heber's place. 'Cost him thirty thousand dollars. You ever hear of such a thing? A man putting thirty thousand good dollars into

17

a place to eat and sleep?'

Jud, thinking of the hundred thousand dollar estates in upstate New York, merely turned his little liquor glass in its own dampness and said nothing.

For a moment neither of them said anything, then Buck Loring, poking his middle with two fingers, ground out, 'I'll kill Brownell if it's the last thing I ever do.'

Jud looked up, his bold blue eyes amused again. 'It just might be the last thing you ever do,' he said. 'How'd he get your gun away from you?'

'Hit me from behind. We were finished talkin' I thought. He started past, then spun around and hit me.'

Jud's amusement dwindled. 'That's the oldest trick in the book,' he said, beginning to feel a little contempt for the rangeman. 'Even little boys don't get caught by that any more.'

Buck's cheek darkened with colour. He had heard the scorn. 'Where I come from folks use guns when they fight.'

'Where's that?'

'Texas!'

Jud viewed the slighter man steadily; all his life he'd been hearing that Texans were a breed apart. He looked away, out over the crowded room, when he said, 'Buck; when you're going to fight—don't talk—just light in.'

Loring watched Jud's eyes roam over the

saloon. 'Where *you* from?' he queried.

'New York—and other places.'

Loring's eyes dropped back to the table. He did not as a rule like Northerners—Yankees— but this big man at his side did not act like a Yankee. Finally he said, 'What brought you to the Dakotas, anyway? Most folks got better sense'n to come out here.'

Jud's roving glance swung back and around. 'Curiosity,' he murmured. Then he smiled again. 'And I like it here.'

'How long you been here?'

'Came in on the morning stage,' said Jud, and laughed aloud at the blank look Buck gave him over this pronouncement. 'Hell; a man doesn't have to grow up in a place to like it.' Jud dumped a coin on the table and arose to stand toweringly. 'Come on; you can show me the sights.'

They went together from saloon to saloon becoming increasingly oiled as they progressed up one side of Front Street then down the other side. Buck Loring knew all the cattlemen they encountered and a good many other people as well. He was treated by those who knew him with a respect that did not escape Jud. He wondered about this until, in a dive called The Golden Slipper, he asked a grizzled drinker just what, exactly, was so special about his new friend. The older man turned a faded steady stare upon Jud and muttered through his ten

19

days' growth of beard one word: 'Gunman.'

For some reason this designation popped in Jud's brain like a whipcrack. He turned heavily to gaze upon animated, flush-faced Buck Loring. Gunman? Why hell; he wasn't hardly old enough or big enough to carry a gun. Still, there was that fine-boned litheness, that subtle gracefulness. Jud faced away and slightly wagged his big head. Texas gunfighter—then how the devil had Brownell disarmed him? He nudged Buck, turned insistently towards him, drawing his attention away from the men he was joking with, saying thickly, 'Buck; something's botherin' me. How come you didn't shoot Brownell when you had the chance?'

Loring squinted in an effort to recollect something, or concentrate, or both, then his face cleared. 'No gun,' he exclaimed. 'He had no gun on him—that louse. Hey; we need another drink. Hey, bartender—two more down here. Hey, Jud; 'want you to meet couple friends of mine. . . .'

'Wait a minute. Dammit, Buck, wait a minute. Let me get this straight. You want to fight a man but because he's got no gun you don't fight him. What kind of sense does that make I'd like to know.'

Loring's brows drew down, his gun-metal eyes studied big Jud Parker over a long moment of silence, then he muttered, 'Hell man; you don't shoot unarmed folks. Not even in the

20

lousy Dakotas folks don't do that.' Loring cleared his throat, still staring. 'I think you're drunk,' he said. 'Come on; let's get out of here and find some hay to bed down in.' He took Jud's arm and started doorward. They made it out into the purple night and Jud, his mind swept briefly clear of fumes by fresh air, halted to draw himself fully upright, adjust his silk hat, smooth out his coat, and step down blindly into the black roadway. He was striding forward with the stiff erectness of a drunk who was concentrating upon keeping to a steady course. He did not see the chestnut team nor the whirling bright yellow wheels of the on-coming rig; he did not even hear Buck Loring's squeal of alarm nor feel his quick tug.

Then the near horse struck him, half turning him, and the buggy collided solidly with his big frame and somewhere, through dull pain and a quick breathlessness, Jud heard a woman's high scream.

He was falling. It seemed ages before he struck down into the dust. Overhead a horse reared and a man's voice called out something in a reedy tone. Then blackness came.

CHAPTER THREE

Jud did not at first recognise Buck Loring's youthful-looking face when he opened his eyes. Beyond Buck was a milling mob of men staring down at him. He thought someone had attacked him; it was a logical enough conclusion for except for one or two of all those faces, he had never before seen so many unkempt, hard, bearded and weathered countenances in one crowd before in his life. He made as though to arise. Buck's hand upon his chest held him down. They had carried him to the edge of a plankwalk but he was still lying in the dirt.

Then he saw the girl's face.

She was kneeling at his side, just beyond Buck. Her eyes seemed blacker than midnight. They were roundly huge and staring. Her nose was slightly tilted at its ending and her mouth below it was large and lovely with a heavy centre fullness to the lower lip. She was, Jud saw even through the fog which plagued him right then, stunningly handsome. He blinked at her; she was attired in something white with lace on it. She obviously was not a saloon girl—then who was she; where had she come from?

He got an arm under, bent and levered himself partially upright. Buck and the beautiful girl both quickly put arms behind his

22

shoulders to sustain him. There was a stab of sharp pain along his right side.

'Damn,' he muttered, and gasped.

'Lie still,' the girl said, then twisted quickly to look behind her. 'Luce,' she said to a nattily dressed man leaning forward. 'Find something to move him on. A stretcher or something.' The well-dressed man faded out through the crowd.

'Give me a hand,' Jud said to Buck, his head entirely clear now. 'Help me up.'

Loring moved to comply but the girl bent over saying, 'No; you're hurt. Wait until the stretcher comes then we'll take you to the doctor.'

'Doctor be damned,' he ground out through clenched teeth. 'Help me up!'

They did so, but others had to step up and aid them because a limp Jud Parker was more than any two people could lift by themselves. When he was standing there wide-legged, weaving like a tree in a high wind, he said to Buck Loring, 'Who did it; where is he?'

'You walked into my buggy,' said the girl, her shoulder sagging beneath the weight of Jud's left arm where she supported him. 'The horses struck you, turning you around into the buggy.'

'I didn't see any running lights.'

The girl bit her lip. 'They weren't lighted, Mister. . . .'

Jud growled at Buck on his right side. 'Easy, confound it. There's a busted rib down there

23

somewhere.'

'Please,' said the girl, 'help me with him to my rig. I'll drive him to the doctor.'

They got Jud to the buggy and up into it. It was a struggle because by this time Jud was actually doing nothing to help himself. He was very conscious of the girl's arm around him and of her shoulder and thigh brushing him as they moved along. His head and vision were totally clear now and he could see how beautiful she was. When she got into the rig at his side there was scarcely room for them both. Again he was alive to their touching bodies.

Buck held up the lines saying, 'I'll tell Shaeffer you've taken him down to Doc's place.'

As they were moving off Jud asked: 'Who is Shaeffer?'

She replied without looking around at him. 'The gentleman I was with when we hit you, Mister. . . .' She turned then to gaze fully upon him. 'Do you mind telling me your name?'

'No'm. It's Jud Parker. Mind if I ask yours?'

'Sharon Caldwell.'

'Nice name,' he murmured, his mind immediately relating this name to another. 'Are you related to Heber Caldwell?'

'His daughter, Mister Parker. We were coming back to town from delivering some papers for my father when we ran into you.' The liquid black eyes remained on his face. 'I just can't tell you how sorry I am I hurt you.

24

Whatever the doctor charges I'll be glad to pay. It was my fault for not having Luce light the carbides—and I'm terribly annoyed with myself.'

Jud made a rueful slow smile at her. It made his rugged face handsome, and as there had always been something contagious about big Jud Parker's smiles, Sharon Caldwell smiled back at him, also ruefully, then she said, 'And your white shirt is torn and your coat too, Mister Parker.'

He turned to inspecting himself. He was dishevelled all right. His silk hat was missing too. To hell with it he told himself, and beat dust from his clothing, righted his coat and ran bent fingers through his curly thatch of dark hair. He stopped setting himself to rights only when the rig drew in before a white picket fence and halted. Then he squinted outward at the darkened house beyond. There was a sign before this house which stated in black Spencerian letters that this was the residence of Doctor Castleton Spence, M.D.

Sharon Caldwell alighted. Jud watched her go around the rig and up to the house. He made no move to alight, himself, but assessed her figure lingeringly as she passed along. She was a large girl, perhaps five and a half feet tall, with a supple grace and a prominent fullness at breast and hip. He sighed; it was good for a change to see a woman whose bust wasn't laced down modestly or was smaller than it should be for the rest of her. He watched her standing there on Doctor Castleton Spence's porch. A woman like this one could take a man's mind off just about anything. He drew back a big breath and winced.

She returned to the rig saying as he offered his hand to help her up, 'There is no one home, apparently, Mister Parker.' She settled in close to him looking uncertain. He was watching her profile and offered no solution; said nothing at all which might have helped her in fact, until she leaned to take up the driving lines.

'Just drive,' he told her. 'The night air is working some of the pain out.'

They drove, mostly in silence. She was, he knew, becoming acutely conscious of him on the seat at her side. They passed beyond Seward City, past miners' shacks and slag-heaps upon hillside shoulders. Around them there was a great depth of silence and overhead a good spring moon shone. Finally he said, 'We'd better go back now, Miss Sharon. It's getting late.' He said this slowly, softly. 'I don't want to keep you out too late. I'll be all right.'

'But your side should be cared for,' she exclaimed. Then, brightening, she added: 'Perhaps Doctor Spence will be home by now.'

'Yes,' he murmured, wishing with all his heart this would not be true. Then, as she swung the rig and started back, he said, 'Have

26

you lived here all your life, Miss Sharon?'

'Most of it, Mister Parker,' she told him, concentrating upon her driving. 'We came here from Illinois—from Chicago—right after my mother died. I was just a child then.'

'But you weren't educated here.'

'No; I went to school in St. Louis.' She turned, saying this, and the buggy wheel struck a boulder, ground up over it and struck down hard on the far side. Jud was shaken; pain flamed in his side and he grunted, reaching with both hands to ease the jar. Sharon instantly halted, twisting towards him, leaning with tenderness as though she also felt anguish.

'I'm so sorry,' she murmured. 'Here; let me help. . . .'

Her arm slid easily behind him as though to aid in re-settling him on the seat. He stiffened at this contact, pain forgotten, and swung around. Their eyes were only inches apart. His left arm moved out, caught her at the waist and swayed her into him. She glimpsed very briefly the hard, dark cut of his big shoulders blotting out the sky, then the lowering sweep of his head. His mouth sought her lips, found them and bore down with a sudden hard and cruel insistence. He enclosed her with his other arm, great muscles bulging with effort.

She twisted in his grip, writhed against him, sought to bring up her hands to strike him, to push him off, to protect herself from his

27

bruising forcefulness. Then his mouth became gentler, moving with a velvet softness upon the surfaces of her lips, still fired with the resolve, the hot run of his hunger, but tender now, and turning soft.

Initially her own lips had been tight-closed and cold with surprise, with fear and near panic. Her wide-open eyes, blacker by shades than they had ever before been in her life, were glazed with terror. He hurt her; but after a moment, when something fierce and scalding was born in her, she was conscious only of the exquisiteness of this pain.

Blood raced upwards from the pit of her stomach to burn her cheeks, mist her vision and roar in her head. Then she let her mouth slacken, the lips part, suddenly wanton and unashamedly seeking. There was, then, more than acquiescence, there was utter and abandoned surrender. All her nerves were crying out their instinctive demands; her body surged upwards suddenly, fully against him, tremblingly eager.

Then he released her.

This sudden parting, so cold and ruthless, left her hanging there briefly, leaning against him with her heart wildly pumping in its secret place, her eyes closed and her bruised mouth ajar.

A sharp sting of dazzling light came past her lids searingly. She flung open both eyes. He was sitting there lighting a cigar, his strong face a bronze mask. Then the match faded, he cast it aside, sucked back a great gust of smoke so that she could hear the deep sweep of it passing down into his lungs, and he smiled at her.

'I guess we better get back,' he said very calmly, eyes twinkling, his handsome mouth curled around the cigar. 'Your daddy'll be worrying about you.' He leaned, took up the lines and flicked them. He was smiling; Sharon did not think she had ever seen such a cruel face in her entire lifetime. 'You want to go back, don't you?'

'Yes,' she breathed. 'Oh yes!'

They only spoke once or twice more. He asked directions to her father's house, and when they finally arrived there he stopped the buggy and sat a moment pensively gazing at the magnificence of Heber Caldwell's mansion.

'Which is your room?' He asked, in a tone which sounded indifferently possessive.

'That one,' she responded, pointing timidly at a second-storey window. She could not force herself to look at him again, but she knew he was smiling down at her.

He alighted, held forth the lines, and said, 'Goodnight, Sharon Caldwell.'

He passed behind the rig, his thrusting stride carrying him well along towards the yonder roadway, each footfall grinding iron-like into the flinty earth. Then even the echoes faded out.

She did not stir for a long time. Not until an old man holding aloft a carriage lantern came shuffling from the rear yard shadows peering from moist eyes up at her.

'You all right, Miss Sharon?'

'I'm all right, Mose.'

'Your paw was frettin'.' The old man shifted the lantern, held up a wrinkled hand and assisted her to alight. 'I expect he's to-bed by now, but an hour or so back he was all in a bother wonderin' what'd 'come of you. Mister Luce come by an' told what'd happened in town.'

'Take care of the team, will you, Mose?'

'Yes'm. Of course.' The lantern swung closer. 'You plumb certain you're all right, Miss Sharon?'

'Yes. I'm fine, Mose. Goodnight.'

'Goodnight, ma'm.'

She swept swiftly up to the house, groped for a side-door latch, found it, then straightened upright very slowly and stood there watching the old retainer lead the horses away.

Around her was the full hush of night, the subtle fragrance of flowers, trees, and night moistness. Where the pewter moon rode in its great-vaulted setting of cold little stars, was a muted and ageless promise for mankind. It was to her as though the night held her cradled in its arms offering solace and sad promise.

She knew.

She knew as surely as she had ever known anything that Jud Parker had not burst upon her awareness this night to be lost in the tumult of this swelling, brawling land. She knew absolutely that she would see him again, and this was what kept her standing there.

What could she say to him; how could she force herself to look into his face again; his cruel, laughing, ruggedly handsome face with its wide mouth and steely jaw and lawless stare.

He knew a secret no one else had yet plumbed. He had found it out through forcefulness, through savagery. The next time their eyes met he would be silently laughing at her as he laughed at her this night when she had freely, fiercely offered herself to him—and he had turned away to casually light a cigar.

'God,' she said into the still, benign night, 'I could kill him.'

Tears scalded her eyes, the night blurred out and she ran into the house fighting back the sobs that racked her from head to toe.

CHAPTER FOUR

The broken rib made sleeping difficult but aside from that Jud was only mildly inconvenienced by it. It was not the first such injury he'd had and he philosophically opined to himself it would probably not be the last of this kind of hurt he'd endure.

What bothered him much more was the condition of his clothing after the accident. He had only this one Prince Albert coat and the best efforts of Seward City's tailor had not been entirely up to disguising the rip his accident had caused to this garment. Still, he said to himself as he went to supper at the Seward House Hotel the second night in town, he was making progress.

He could not have defined this progress, exactly, just yet, nevertheless he had the solid feeling of achievement which went with accomplishment, incomplete though this accomplishment might be.

He ordered supper and sat back with all his muscles loose thoroughly enjoying himself. He ate his meal when it came and afterwards remained at the table to light and savour a strong cigar, watching people pass into and out of the hotel dining-room. Restlessness bubbled in him as it usually did when he was nibbling at the edge of an idea, and the meal, which had been quite good, left him stimulated and replete.

His eyelids lay close together with shrewd lines appearing at his temples; his thoughts, behind half-closed bold eyes, formed and re-formed patterns which, while as yet incomplete, were nonetheless worthwhile.

He kept returning to the discovery he'd made the evening before: that Heber Caldwell's lovely daughter was hungry for love. Why this should be he could shrewdly guess. In this land of women-starved men so truly exquisite a girl would ordinarily have queues of eligible bachelors at her doorway night and day. She could go to supper or buggy riding in the moonlight with a different suitor every night of the year. Why then was this not so with Sharon Caldwell? Because, he told himself, her father being the kind of a man he obviously was, trusted no one to be honest about his daughter even though she was as beautiful a girl as one could find west of the Missouri, or east of it either for that matter.

He stirred in his chair recalling other events of the night before. The transplanted Texan, Buck Loring; that big freighter, Brownell, with his hating small eyes and fierce dark beard. The multitude of voices in all those saloons, the smells and jostlings and the feelings they had evoked in him. The sound of some unseen woman's laughter. Then back to Sharon Caldwell again, and his carefully sequenced thoughts of her.

What was it that drew a man's thoughts always to women; maybe it was the hungers that built up in a man as he knocked around in life, moving like the needle of a compass towards that one woman who must inevitably sear her impressions forever in a man's mind, upon his heart and soul. Maybe it was the awareness men had even in their languid moments of women moving around them, such as the woman who now entered the dining-room as Jud Parker leaned forward in his chair preparatory to arising from the table, all his attention suddenly closing down upon her.

She was in her twenties with hair so deeply red it was the colour of burnished copper. There was a roundness to her body that sang over the room to him, exciting all his male instincts. Her face was handsome; the mouth was strong, almost masculinely wilful, and her greeny eyes were cool, her manner poised and indifferent.

He stood there watching her. As she and her escort, an elderly, withered and stringy man with a gash for a mouth and very pale, very calculating, very icy eyes, went to a table and sat down. He saw how her head lifted slightly as she threw outward a bold appraisal of other diners, then their eyes met and held. She didn't look away; her stare was as bold and lawless as was his. It was as though she were challenging him to break the composure of her face. As though, bored and indifferent, she was looking for something to break this boredom.

She knew she was beautiful too; that also was in her stare—in her poise and deep calm. Her eyes told him as much. They also, as the moments slid by, told him that she knew him to be a full man as other men also were, with the same impulses. Her stare did not rebuke him so much as it simply scorned him. Then, as he began to move doorward, his big, powerful shoulders swinging, he saw a break of interest appear in her eyes. He smiled to himself and moved on out of the dining-room.

Buck Loring was passing along the roadway in company with three other horsemen as Jud stepped out upon the rough board walkway. He let off a high rangeman's yell at sight of Jud which caused many heads to turn, numbers of eyes to go swiftly to the big man and linger there. Then Loring wheeled in close and swung down, flung his reins to one of his friends and stepped up to Jud with a boyish grin.

'Whatever happened to you last night? After you'n Miss Sharon drove off I went over to Doc Spence's place, but there wasn't any sign of you.'

Jud shrugged saying only, 'I took her home then went to my room.' He touched Loring's arm and half twisted from the waist. 'In the dining-room there, an old man and a chestnut-haired filly came in. Go take a look at her then tell me if you know her.'

Loring dutifully departed, was gone only moments, then returned with a broad smile. 'Sure I know her, Jud. That there is Miss Mary Alice Curry.' Loring's twinkling eyes turned a little smoky. 'You know who that is with her?'

'No.'

'Heber Caldwell.' Loring added some strong epithets to the banker's name, then said, 'Come on; I'm dry as a bag of bones.' He took Jud's arm and flung over his shoulder at the other riders: 'Hey; you fellers look after the horses.'

They entered the Warbonnet Saloon and bellied up to the bar.

'Who is Mary Alice Curry?' Jud asked.

'Old Heber's merciless right arm, that's who,' said the cowman, wig-wagging for drinks. 'He hatches the meanness an' she sees that the things are done.'

'You mean she works at his bank?'

'Sure. Hell; don't women work in the banks in New York?'

'Well,' said Jud, struggling to recall ever seeing a woman working in a New York City bank. 'I guess they do. Only she's almighty pretty to be working in a bank.'

Loring hooted at this, tossed off his first drink, and twinkled a merry look at the giant beside him. 'You wouldn't get within a mile of her—not Miss Mary Alice. Nossir. She's got quicksilver for blood. She hates men, unless of course they're like old Heber and don't consider her a woman at all.'

Jud picked up his glass, soberly gazed down into it and said, 'There's not a man living who'd look on her as something besides a female woman, Buck.'

Again Loring made his hooting laugh. 'Old Heber does.'

'I said a man,' growled Jud, and downed his drink.

Buck suddenly slumped against the bar, his eyes fixed in powerful thought upon the oily circlet of liquid under his empty glass. Finally he straightened back saying, 'By God I'm willing to spend twenty dollars to see you try'n cousin-up to Miss Mary Alice.' He fished from a trouser pocket some crumpled bills, peeled off one and began searching among the crowd in the Warbonnet for a face. When he finally found it he called loudly over the saloon's steady drone.

'Hey, Charley; come here a minute.'

A lean, slightly drunk range rider came over and stopped. He gazed upon Jud for a moment, then gravely nodded, saying aside to Buck, 'He's big enough to eat hay. 'You want me to saddle and ride him?'

Buck laughed. 'This here is Jud—Jud Something-or-other.'

'Parker,' said Jud.

'Yeah, this here is Jud Parker, Charley. Jud, this here is Charley Ringo.'

Jud dutifully shook hands with the weaving rider. Ringo made a little smile and gallantly half-bowed.

'Hey, Charley,' resumed Buck, 'you took Miss Mary Alice buggy ridin' one time didn't you?'

'I did,' replied Ringo with what Jud thought was a hint of loftiness to his tone.

'Well now, Charley, I'm goin' to give you twenty dollars if you'll get her into a buggy again and take her north o' town about a mile.'

'What for?' Ringo asked, beginning to frown at Buck.

'Big Jud here thinks she's a real woman.'

Ringo looked wide-eyed at Jud. 'He does? Well, by golly he needs eye-spectacles then, is all I got to say.'

Buck held up the twenty dollar bill. 'Can you get her to go ridin' with you?'

Ringo considered the money. When he replied, however, it was evident to Jud that his masculine charm had been challenged before strangers and this even more than the twenty dollars was what prompted his brief nod and answer.

'Sure she'll go buggy-ridin' with me—even if she is a regular icicle.' Ringo reached forth, plucked away the twenty dollar bill, then squinted at Loring. 'What you two got hatched up, anyway?'

'After you park north o' town I and Jud'll happen to come ridin' along. After that you and I'll just move off a piece and watch Jud here try'n make the grade with her.'

Jud touched Buck's arm. 'Wait a minute,' he said. 'I didn't say I wanted to. . . .'

'Look-a-here,' hooted Loring. 'He's trying to

crawfish.'

Ringo teetered back on his heels to gaze up into Jud's face. He muttered something but neither Jud nor Buck could distinguish what it was. Then Ringo began shaking his head in a dolorous fashion.

'Crawfish hell,' growled Jud. 'But this is silly. What'll I say to her? Anyway, I didn't say I wanted to know her.'

'You said any man'd look on her as a female woman, didn't you?'

'Sure, but hell. . . .'

Loring laughed a little scornfully. 'In this country a man puts up or shuts up, Jud.' He caught Charley Ringo's attention saying, 'Go on, Charley. She's at the hotel having supper with old Caldwell. We'll give you an hour then we'll follow along.'

'I have no horse,' muttered Jud, scowling.

'Have another drink,' exclaimed Loring. 'You're goin' to need it. Don't worry about a horse, I'll get you one. I'll get you a dozen of 'em, in fact, just to see you try an' get a smile out o' Miss Mary Alice. Hey, bartender, two refills down here; come on man, shake a leg.'

Jud bent on the Texan a long, slow look. He was beginning to wonder what it was about Buck Loring he'd found interesting the night before. Loring was like a mid-teen farm boy; his sense of humour was rude and half developed.

He considered telling Buck to go to hell, then

39

turning on his heel and striding out of the saloon. But after the second drink he grew thoughtful. Loring was thus far his only friend in Seward City; besides, Loring was going to be useful to him. He knew this because he'd already, at supper and earlier, begun to work out an idea. After the third drink—and he stopped there this night—he began remembering Mary Alice Curry, and as ridiculous as Loring's half-baked scheme was, it offered Jud at least another opportunity to see her.

In the end Jud shook his head over what was in prospect but said no more against it. This heightened Buck Loring's anticipatory good nature and they progressed from saloon to saloon with Buck drinking and Jud abstaining until they encountered two of the three other rangemen Loring had ridden into town with. Then the final plans were made, the use of a saddle mount was secured for Jud, and Buck finally led him out into the soft-scented night to a hitchrail where a drowsing big buckskin horse stood hipshot-patient.

'How much time's Charley had?' demanded Loring, having some trouble with his legs.

'A little more than an hour.'

'Then let's go,' cried Buck, making for another saddled animal at the rack.

Jud, watching the cowman get astride, began to doubt very much if a girl such as Mary Alice

Curry would go buggy riding with a man such as Charley Ringo had appeared to be.

'This is a waste of time,' he told Loring, as he unlooped the buckskin's reins, turned the beast out into the roadway and stepped across him. 'She won't be out there.'

'Got twenty dollars to bet on that?' challenged Loring. ''Cause I sure have. She'll be there all right.'

'How do you know that?'

Buck wheeled away from the hitchrail and eased his animal out into a long-legged walk. Looking over his shoulder at Jud he said, 'Because Charley's worked for her—and old Caldwell—and she'll be curious about what he wants.'

'Does Caldwell have cattle?'

Buck exaggeratedly wagged his head. 'He's got no livestock an' wants none. He only wants to own them of us as sweats and freezes working livestock so he can squeeze the guts out o' us. Ringo's hired out his gun a few times to help Caldwell evict miners and others.'

Jud, recalling the hatchet-faced, lean and blank-eyed Charley Ringo, filed this information away and urged his mount to catch up with Buck Loring's animal. In this fashion, side by side, they passed northward out of Seward City.

CHAPTER FIVE

After they had passed well beyond town Jud made a slow swing to search the roundabout shadows. There was only night-hush around them. It was another of those pleasant spring nights with a high wash of stars overhead and the singing curve of heaven continuing to its dim merging with earth.

At his side Buck Loring rode along humming to himself but when they'd nearly covered the allotted mile Buck became quietly watchful.

'Gotta be somewhere hereabouts,' he muttered, straining to plumb the gloom around them.

'Unless he didn't get her to go with him,' said Jud, half hoping this was so.

Loring drew fully upright in the saddle saying triumphantly, 'There! Yonder's the rig beside that juniper tree.'

Jud, riding easily, comfortably, until this moment doubting they'd encounter the rig and with the ease of a long day's ending upon him, roused up to peer ahead. Loring was correct; a liverybarn top-buggy with a drowsing animal in the shafts stood darkly on ahead. He sighed; somehow that unprepossessing Charley Ringo had gotten Mary Alice Curry to accompany him. It made him tentatively revise his earlier opinion of the handsome woman with the titian hair.

'Go on,' said Buck, reining down to a halt. 'It's your play.' He was widely grinning.

Jud kept on riding. He approached the top-buggy from the west, cutting around it so as to appear on the passenger's side. As he hove into sight he saw a lanky figure get down and stand motionless watching him. A cigarette's sullen crimson tip glowed, then faded. Finally the tinny voice of Ringo said, 'Mary Alice, this here is a friend of mine—Jud Parker.' Ringo turned casually, indifferently, and walked around behind the rig, took hold of Jud's reins as the big man stepped out and down, and walked off southerly leading the animal. Jud paced forward.

Mary Alice was sitting erectly, her lips flattened and her eyes coolly watchful. When she looked directly at him Jud saw the lovely turning of her throat. She was entirely on guard; not so much afraid of him as alert to his presence and sceptical of his intentions. She said at once, 'Why didn't you just come over to the table?' She was studying his face closely where he stood beside the rig less than arm's distance from her. 'I would have thought you'd have managed an introduction differently than this.'

He said: 'What makes you so sure I wanted an introduction?'

She did not answer and he moved around the horse, got heavily up into the buggy and leaned

43

back, half-turned so as to face her. Her attention closed down upon him. Even in the shadows he sighted the sturdy beating of an erratic pulse in her throat. He smiled at her without much mirth. Her eyes narrowed in appraisal, then opened wider.

'What do you want with me? Who are you?'

'My name's Jud Parker. I didn't particularly want anything with you. I just told some friends of mine I thought you were a real woman.'

She looked quickly away from him, out over the horse's still back into the far-away night. He went on talking; she listened to his voice, weighing it, suspicious of him and possibly, finally, a little bit fearful.

'I'm new here in Seward City. I'm a mite lonesome. When I saw you in the hotel dining-room with your father I said to myself you'd be worth knowing.'

'That wasn't my father, that was Mr. Caldwell.' She swung her gaze back to his face. 'I think you're lying,' she said. 'There are women in the saloons, Mister Parker.'

He reached for the lines, unlooped them from round the whip-socket and clucked at the horse. As the buggy lurched forward he said, 'That kind of woman never held my interest very long, Mary Alice, not even when I was a young buck with a bow in my neck.'

He turned the buggy in a big circle and headed it back towards town. From the edge of his vision he saw her relax at this, lean back against the upholstery with most of the tightness leaving her lips.

'All right,' she eventually said, her tone altered away from hardness, 'you've met me. Now what?'

'Supper tomorrow night to start with.'

'Then what?'

He turned. 'How would I know? In this game the woman holds the initiative, not the man.'

She said: 'You're big enough to force the issue, Mister Parker.'

He chuckled at her, his eyes for the first time twinkling genuine amusement at her. 'Folks live life by certain rules, Mary Alice. It's not gentlemanly not to abide by them.'

Her voice came at him now with a lift of interest.

'Tell me, Mister Parker, do you always abide by the rules?'

He knew without turning aside that she was intently watching him. The smile lingered down around his mouth. 'When it's convenient I do,' he murmured. 'Do you?'

'Usually.'

He swung his head, drew back on the lines to halt the rig, and sat there considering her. Finally he said, 'You in a hurry to get back?'

Her reply came over an interval of silence. 'No great hurry, I guess. What did you have in mind?'

'Just a little drive. It's a wonderful night.'

'Yes,' she said. 'I hope Charley Ringo finds it so.'

He smiled without speaking, took up the lines again and started the livery animal off slowly on a diverging tangent which took them out around Seward City southward.

'Mind if I smoke, Mary Alice?'

'No.'

He lit a cigar, settled it between his teeth, big mouth thoughtfully curled around it, and drove along without speaking for a long time. Mary Alice, piqued by this long silence, his slouched posture and apparent thoughtfulness, ultimately said, 'What brought you to Seward City?'

'Curiosity. I heard about it back in St. Joe.'

'Is that where you're from?'

'No.'

'Well; do you have a trade?'

'Several trades, Mary Alice.' He looked over at her. 'Your mother should've raised you differently,' he murmured.

'What do you mean?'

'All those personal questions.'

Lights danced in her tawny eyes as they met and held his gaze. Her mouth was lying gently closed now with all the earlier tension gone from it. There remained, though, a trace of her former distrust and reserve as she studied him, but beyond that he saw the fullness waiting. The fullness was a promise and a temptation to him.

46

It brought up again his steady, slow and knowing smile.

She instantly recognised the recklessness in this smile of his, and for all the nearly irresistible contagion of his smiles, she did not alter expression one iota. She watched him and understood him and her expression continued smoothly calculating and interested—yet distant. But there was a tell-tale revelation of how she *really*, inwardly felt, and he saw it: the quick lifting of her breasts with disturbed breathing. A confused and confusing warmth ran between them in the buggy, a swift and common knowledge.

She dropped her glance.

He held the cigar away and eyed it, then resumed his smoking and driving, thinking privately that he had met her unflinching challenge twice now, once in the dining-room, and just now in the rig, and the second meeting had been his triumph: She had looked away. His lips curled roughly upwards at their outer corners. The most seasoned woman in the world could not long face the nakedness of a man's total want when he let it fully show in his stare.

'Tell me about yourself,' he quietly stated. As before—with Sharon Caldwell—indifferent, slightly contemptuous after tearing away that outer shield and viewing in each of these two women what lay trembling beyond. In the continuing, same cruel tone he said, 'What is it that keeps you aloof from men?'

'You just named it,' she exclaimed, her displeasure with him roughening her otherwise deep and husky voice. 'Men!'

'No,' he retorted slowly, squinting into the night beyond the head of the horse. 'It may be that you think miners are dirty, that freighters smell of cookfires and sweat, that the rangemen are rough and uncouth. But you want *a* man, Mary Alice. You want one as bad as ever any woman wanted one.'

The bluntness of this statement brought a break of surprise to her features; it arrested her mood, checking it up hard. She faced towards him with a close and wondering attention. 'I suppose you're that man,' she huskily said.

'I could be.'

'Not in a thousand years you couldn't be.'

'All right,' he said indifferently. 'Maybe not me, but he'll come along someday, and he won't be some old fool with all the juices dried out of him either.' He turned to look at her; to study the way her lips lay parted now, her eyes wide and shiny as though burning with unshed tears, and he concluded with: 'You'd better start looking for him, too, Mary Alice. Nothing's as good as we think it should be, and time has a way of passing us by.'

She had temper; he saw it come now to her face and lips; watched her beautiful tawny eyes narrow and lose their warmth, and harden

48

against him.

'Hell,' he growled, halting the rig again, taking down the cigar and tossing it away and reaching roughly for her with the same continuing sweep of big arms. 'Enough of this.'

She fought him. When he pinioned her arms and bent her back feeling for her mouth she arched against him, her breath breaking harshly upon his face. Then he had her mouth under his.

He held her thus, rigid in his embrace, for a long time, his fire engulfing them. She did not yield until the very last instant. Then he released her arms; they went up fiercely to encircle his neck and hold him passionately to her. Fire came up out of her to match his own fire and this time, drawing back eventually, he found himself shaken by the drowning possessiveness which she had unleashed against him.

This was no girl with her first tender stirrings. This was a wilful woman who knew her mind and her hunger.

Nor did Mary Alice Curry hang there, eyes closed, bruised lips tremulous. She met his hot stare with a glare as demanding as his own look, and instead of remaining breathlessly silent, she said, 'Maybe you are the man, Jud Parker. You just might be.'

She pushed the lines into his hands then raised the back of one hand to her lips, let it linger there while she savoured the lingering pain.

'Drive,' she commanded.

He drove.

This had never before happened to him. She was a woman equally as cruel as he was, equally as demanding, as wilful, as iron-like in her resolve and her ambition.

'Can you imagine what it's like working for a dehydrated old man, a widower, whose eyes follow you every instant; whose mind constantly dreams of what he'd have done to you thirty years earlier and whose sly remarks never let you forget it?'

'You mean Caldwell?'

'Yes,' she breathed vehemently, in her turmoil overlooking the fact that he'd mentioned a name that in a calmer moment would have put her on guard against him. 'Yes. Heber Caldwell. I can't relax around him, not for an instant. It's been this way for two years.' She ceased speaking, drew back a quivering breath, then rushed on. 'He only thinks of two things. Money and me.'

'They tell me he has enough money.'

'He'll never have enough; he'll go to his grave scheming ways to make more.'

'With mortgages?'

'Mortgages and liens and loans, buying and selling. Right now he's working on a way to corner the hay market.'

'They don't raise much hay hereabouts,' said Jud, tooling the rig back towards Seward City, his night-shadowed face hidden from her so that she failed to notice the gradually narrowing of his calculating eyes.

'That's the point. Right now in the spring of the year the freighters and stockmen have plenty of grass. In the late summer, fall and winter they'll need hay. He'll have it all tied up with options by then.'

'So he can hike the price per ton?'

'Yes, exactly.'

Jud flicked the lines, the horse broke over into a shambling trot, and the orange pinpricks of lamplight where Seward City lay dead ahead, began to grow larger.

'What else does he do to make money?'

But Mary Alice's vehemence was passing; she was spent and drained of emotion and leaned back the rest of the way into town, eyes closed, shallowly breathing, saying nothing.

He took her home, returned the rig to the livery-barn, then went along the roadway as far as the wooden bench outside the town marshal's office, and there sank down to be alone with his forming thoughts.

CHAPTER SIX

It was nearly midnight when he roused himself to go in search of Buck Loring. He did not at once encounter the rangeman but he did come upon Charley Ringo, no drunker now than he had been three hours earlier although he obviously had been steadily tanking up since then. Ringo nodded gravely at Jud saying, 'I wouldn't have believed it.'

'Believed what?' demanded Jud.

'You got lip-rouge on your face, Mister Parker.'

'Have you seen Loring?'

'Not in the last hour I ain't.'

Jud continued his search and ultimately located Buck at the Warbonnet. He prised him away from the bar, took him to a darkened corner and pushed him down into a chair.

'Do you raise hay?' he asked Loring without preliminaries.

'Hay? Sure I raise hay. Well; not *raise* it exactly. It grows volunteer in these parts. But I put it up for winter feed. Hey, Jud; isn't that lip-rouge on your cheek?'

'Who else raises it hereabouts?'

Loring wetly blinked; he was well along towards inebriation. 'Lip-rouge?' he said. 'Hardly anyone that I know of.'

'Hay. Who else raises hay, dammit?'

'Me'n one or two others. That's 'bout all because that's about all the cowmen in these parts. In the summertime Texas herds come up here. But them fellers sell out and leave as soon as. . . .'

'Do you put up hay for sale or just for your own use?'

'Mostly for my own use. I usually, if it's a good year, put up maybe a hundred tons to sell along with it, though. Peddle it to freighters. Usually in the fall and winter.'

'Do you ever contract it?'

'What?'

'Contract it; sell it before you have it all put up.'

Loring chuckled and shook his head. 'You New York Yankees got a lot to learn. Hell; a man can't sell what he hasn't got. 'Course I don't sell it before I put it up.'

'How much will you put up this year for sale?'

'Been a good wet spring,' said Loring, beginning to fiercely scowl as he tried to concentrate. 'Maybe eighty tons. Maybe a hundred tons. But I can't sell it until. . . .'

'How much will it sell for?'

Loring shrugged. 'Two dollars a ton maybe. At the most three dollars in the stack. Why?'

'I want an option on every blade of it you'll put up this year.'

'An option?'

'I want to buy every ton you'll put up at three dollars a ton. I don't want you to sell a blade of it to anyone else between now and the time you've got it in the stack.'

'Oh,' said Loring. He rubbed a shirtsleeve across his face. 'You goin' in the stock business, Jud?'

'Just the hay business. Well; do I get the option?'

'At three dollars a ton?'

'Yes. Three dollars a ton stacked.'

'All right,' said Buck quietly, gazing steadily at Jud. 'Sure; you can have it. You want this option thing in writing?'

'Yeah. I'll give you fifty dollars to bind it.'

'All right. I'll look you up tomorrow night and sign the paper.'

Jud got up, blew out a big breath and said, 'Come on; I'll buy you a drink and you can tell me who else puts up hay for sale.'

'Sure enough.'

Jud got the names, then took Buck with him when he went in search of these stockmen. He found two of them in town and made them the identical offer he'd made Buck. One of the rangemen was suspicious and asked a lot of questions. But in the end Jud also optioned all the surplus hay these men proposed putting up. He made each of them the identical proposition he'd made Loring, then he left Buck at one of the bars with his friends, returned to his room,

54

counted his money—sixty-six dollars—and laboriously penned the options, hastened back to the cattlemen, secured their signatures by promising to meet them the following night with their advance payments, then went alone back to the Warbonnet, had three stiff drinks to quiet his nerves, and passed out alone into the night.

It was late; too late actually to transact business in the orthodox fashion, but Jud Parker was not orthodox and extremely few of the things he'd done in his lifetime had been orthodox either. He started at once for the residence of Heber Caldwell.

Around him the night lay heavily somnolent; only his thrusting stride shattered it, making eddying-outward echoes as he purposefully made his way west of town to that thirty-acre estate with its magnificent white-painted double-decked house set back under trees in a perpetual soft murk.

He cut up on to Heber Caldwell's cinder driveway passing impatiently along with a solitary glowing lamp within the house as his guiding beacon. When his feet struck down upon the gallery, around back somewhere a big dog boomed and a chain rattled. Jud drew down for a listening moment; the chain quivered at its ending against a steel pole. He faced around again confident the dog was securely tethered, and raised a big fist against Heber Caldwell's front door.

The echoes of that sturdy pounding chased themselves beyond the panel. Jud waited. He had one cigar left and longed to light it. He was nervous and made no attempt to deny this to himself. A man with sixty-six dollars had to be nervous in the home of a man who had hundreds of thousands of dollars, even if he wasn't seeking to perpetrate a bald-faced bluff. He would wait and light the cigar under old Caldwell's nose.

No, dammit, he'd light it now. He did this, cupping the flame and sucking back that biting taste; was in fact standing there, massive head lowered, huge fists up in front of his face, bold and fearless eyes visible above his fingers, when the door opened and a very old man stood there peering wetly up at him. Jud's cold stare lifted, went to the oldster and clung there. He slowly dropped his arms, exhaled, and said, 'Is Mister Caldwell handy?'

The old man, fascinated by Jud's size, his commanding stare and his bold gaze, began to awkwardly form words. 'He's—havin' his nightcap, mister. He don't like to be bothered after supper—and all.'

'And I,' boomed Jud, 'don't like having to transact business in the middle of the night either. Show me in to him.'

This house on the inside was exactly as Jud had pictured it to be. Money had been lavishly spent to make it a kind of monument to its owner and creator. Regardless of cost, of time, even of the sweat and actual blood of many men and animals, its furnishings had been laboriously brought overland or around the Horn; they had teetered upon mules' backs over the Divide; they had filled huge freight wagons, and they had come at last to repose here within these handsome walls, not as items of utility, but as milestones commemorating each successful financial triumph of old Heber Caldwell. There were Persian carpets and Chippendale tables with flawless marble tops. There were medieval chairs of wood so old it was black and glossy to the touch. There were hanging mirrors in a land where not one man in a hundred owned anything even resembling glass; men who shaved—when they shaved at all—beside still mountain pools, or by the distorting images of highly polished reflectors, would have gazed in awe upon these perfect mirrors.

'Who is it?' demanded a harsh voice as Jud's guide stopped at a huge door to scratch upon it with timid fingers.

The old man turned, flustered, for Jud's name. For a second Jud looked into the wet old eyes, then shouldered past, caught the door fastening and flung it inward. Across a sumptuous room lined with books, standing with a wine glass in one claw-like hand near a table with an ornate lamp upon it, was Heber

Caldwell. Jud recognised him at once.

'Who—the devil are you?' Caldwell challenged, stiffening the full length of him at Jud's unceremonious entrance. 'What do you mean bursting in on me like this?'

Jud passed over as far as the table conscious that his size, his abrupt entrance and his silence had given him the advantage. He said, 'My name is Jud Parker. I understand you want to buy hay.'

Caldwell turned fully. His icy, pale eyes ran over Jud then settled coldly upon his face. 'You burst into my house in the middle of the night to try and sell me *hay*!' He shouted. 'Mose! Mose; dammit, throw this man out.'

Jud's bold eyes brightened. His wide mouth drew gently upwards at its far corners. 'You don't have five men in your employ who could do that, Mister Caldwell,' he told the banker, whose darkening face was getting splotchy with wrath. 'Maybe not even ten men. Suppose you sit down and listen.'

'Out!' screeched the enraged banker. 'Out, confound you!'

'Sit down and listen!'

Caldwell's heavy breathing cut the sudden stillness which came to settle between them across the little table. His eyes bulged, his mouth worked. Finally he said, 'Mose! Fetch me a pistol!'

Jud turned from the waist to glare at the old

58

man rooted by the door. 'You just close that door,' he ordered. 'If you bring him a pistol someone's going to get hurt—and Mose—it damned well might be you and Caldwell. Now go on; close the door.'

The door closed.

Caldwell put down his glass of wine. He continued to work his lips but no words came. Jud motioned with one big arm towards a chair.

'Sit down, Mister Caldwell.'

Caldwell did not move. His nostrils quivered; his hands balled into bony fists and he stood there adamantly waiting.

Jud said in the same steely-soft tone: 'I have five hundred ton of hay to sell you. All in the stack.'

'I wouldn't buy a single ton off you,' spat the older man, 'if you had the only hay in the blasted world!'

Jud went on as though Caldwell hadn't spoken. 'You want it to sell to the freighters this winter. I'll sell it to you tonight for ten dollars a ton.'

'*Ten dollars*! Are you insane, man? I can buy hay right here in Seward City for two.'

'No you can't.'

'Yes I can!'

'Mister Caldwell, this is local hay.'

'What of it? I can get all the local hay I want at two dollars.'

'Like hell you can. I have options on every

ton which is to be cut and stacked by the hay producers around Seward City for the balance of this year.'

'*What!*'

Jud produced the signed options. He held them loosely in one big fist, and he made a flinty small smile at Heber Caldwell. Then he tossed them carelessly down upon the little table.

'Ten dollars a ton and it's all yours.'

Caldwell snatched at the papers. He shuffled through them, pale eyes skimming over each sheet of paper, then with a sizzling oath he flung them away from him.

Jud reached down, took a clean wine glass and poured himself a drink from Caldwell's decanter. He lifted the glass to his lips and gazed steadily at the old man. 'To your health,' he murmured, and drained the glass, set it aside, and said, 'Ten dollars a ton, Mister Caldwell. You'll re-sell it this winter for twenty, maybe thirty if you make them starve their animals long enough.'

'Who are you?' Caldwell shrieked. 'What did you say your name was?'

'Jud Parker.'

'Now you listen to me, Jud Parker; I've had men killed for less than what you're trying to do to me.'

'Don't try it with me, Mister Caldwell. I've been in a few fights myself.' Jud's voice dropped, his bleak gaze was fixed with strong intensity upon the banker. 'With me, all I've got to lose is my life. With you. . . .'

'Yes?'

Jud made a gesture around the room. 'Fire would destroy this, Mister Caldwell. Something worse than fire would destroy Miss Sharon. For you—a broken spine and what years you've got left spent in poverty in a wheelchair.'

Heber Caldwell's face paled to a ghastly grey. He groped for the chair nearby and dropped down into it. 'Who are you?' he asked again, in a voice as dry as old corn husks. 'Why are you doing this? Who is behind you?'

Jud answered none of the questions. He said simply, 'Be content with a hundred, perhaps two hundred per cent profit this time, Caldwell.' He bent, retrieved the signed options, smoothed them out and considered them. 'Ten dollars a ton payable here and now and I'll endorse these over to you—and you can still control all the hay around Seward City.'

'I don't have that much money here in the house.'

'That's all right,' said Jud. 'I'll endorse these over to you anyway—then call at the bank in the morning.'

'Then,' croaked Heber Caldwell, his hating, pale eyes slyly brightening, 'sign them and get out.'

Jud endorsed the options, straightened up and turned fully towards Caldwell. 'I'll be at the

61

bank in the morning when it opens,' he said. 'Goodnight.'

CHAPTER SEVEN

Out again in the dark silence Jud walked steadily to the extremity of Caldwell's estate and there, hidden from the house by night-darkness, he did not swing east as he'd come earlier to this spot, he swung west. Softening his tread, moving with a grace rarely seen in a man of his bulk, he cut along through fringing trees until he was back again within six hundred feet of Caldwell's house, and there made himself comfortable.

Lamplight still glowed from Heber Caldwell's study. Jud smiled, imagining the old man's mood. He sought about him for a comfortable seat among the dense pines, found one and let himself gently down. The night was warm, the sky, as much of it as he could make out beyond these stiff-topped trees, was clear and flawless. He anticipated a long wait and was now prepared to endure it.

Moments passed, then the old man who had admitted Jud to Heber Caldwell's house went heavily jogging out of the yard on a big, gentle roan horse. Jud made certain of this rider's identity, then settled back again, smiling. It

62

helped, he said to himself, if you wished to assess another man's reactions, if you were the same kind of a man yourself. Caldwell had sent his retainer for someone. He did not mean to give Jud a penny for his options. He meant to have him severely beaten or perhaps killed. That, thought Jud with approval, was precisely what he himself would have done under reversed circumstances, had he been a fierce old man challenged by a fierce younger man.

Time passed quietly. Jud looked outwards towards the window of Sharon Caldwell. It was dark in that room. He pictured her lying abed with that great wealth of her hair spread upon a snow-white pillow making a frame for the cameo-like fineness of her face. He re-lived the intimate moments they had known and his wide mouth unconsciously, gently, curled into a smile of masculine triumph. If old Heber only knew. . . .

He stirred, considered the big house through the pines and sharpened his thoughts against old Heber. If he'd had the opportunity he might have come up with something even more costly for the banker. But a man with sixty-six dollars doesn't have much time. He thought of what possibly lay ahead this night. He had no gun— had never cared for the things in fact; felt that only simpletons used them, actually, because they could not think beyond force.

He felt his cracked rib. It did not hurt even

when he breathed, but he would remember to shield this side of him if there was violence. He grinned. *If* there was violence. Of course there would be; old Heber's eyes had flamed with the notion of it. He was, like Jud also was, the kind of a man who used violence equally with legal processes to triumph. The difference between this kind of man and the gun-wearing toughs of this far frontier was simply that the prairie pirates, unlike the gun-bearers, never used violence solely for violence's sake; they preferred to intimidate, to overawe, to bully and threaten, to achieve their ends. They understood the delicate balance between force and persuasion. They also understood that those who dealt exclusively in violence inevitably attracted others like them and eventually violence destroyed them.

Old Caldwell would use violence now. Jud was certain of this. He would assume, too, that Caldwell would employ assassination if he had to. In fact he would assume that old Caldwell would stoop to any means to destroy big Jud Parker, and this also Jud approved of. There was no place for ethics in the un-clean battle for money; there never in the world's history had been up to now and Jud was unshakeably convinced there never would be. Ethics were for the gun-fighters, not for the prairie pirates.

He was in perhaps the direst peril he'd ever been in; he alone with perhaps no more than one or two friends, was challenging the ruler of the Dakotas with no holds barred. Instead of feeling fear as a result of his own boldness, he was thrilled by it. A man with nothing and a patched coat had bearded notorious Heber Caldwell in his own home and had seen the old villain's cheeks fall in with trepidation. This, he told himself powerfully, was the way God intended for a man to live!

He'd made thousands of dollars in less than three hours. He didn't have it yet but he'd get it—or they'd bury him; but that was all right; the risk was well worth it and big Jud Parker had never put any very great value on life, his own or anyone else's.

This was the way money was made, he thought. Not with emporiums or livestock or saloons. This way—with violence, with bald-faced bluffs, with a man's brains. With inside information of the big plans of other men.

He came down to earth with a crash.

Mary Alice would hear what he'd done. She'd know how he'd done it too; old Heber might never find out, but Mary Alice would know and she'd hate him for using her. His relishing broad smile dwindled. He had never fought a woman. Where he came from women raised children and demurely sewed or cooked. He reached up slowly to run crooked fingers through his hair. How did a man fight a woman?

A solution presented itself tentatively. Men

65

didn't fight women, they conquered them. They used their embracing arms, their ardent lips, their gentling hands, their smooth lies. But, recollecting Mary Alice Curry's quiet and perceptive acuity he wondered if this could ever be accomplished in her case. Then he smiled again, there in the waiting night; it sure-Lord would be pleasant to find out.

Down the silent night came distantly echoing hoof-falls. He cocked his head gauging distances. When the ridden horses continued in their steadily oncoming approach he got up, dusted his clothing and flexed his great limbs. After a time he could make them out, two bobbing silhouettes. One smaller, wizened, hunched up there astride a big old horse whose colour he knew would be roan. This would be Mose. He turned the fullness of his stare upon old Mose's companion. There was something familiar about this larger, younger man even in the gloom; even atop a saddle animal.

Caleb Brownell, the freighter!

Jud remained motionless long enough to confirm this identity, then cast a searching glance into the darkness beyond. Behind Heber Caldwell's mansion was the stable-house. Here, also glowing whitely because of its white paint, Caldwell's horses were kept and his retainers lived. Also, back there somewhere, was the big dog he'd heard earlier.

He began edging deeper into shadows. Where

night-blackness dripped most heavily upon him, he wheeled to the right making for that other, more distant building. He never did see the dog, but evidently his stealth kept the beast from seeing or scenting him either, for by the time old Mose and Caleb were crunching along over the cinder driveway, Jud was close enough to the stable to flatten behind a gigantic fir tree watching their approach. He heard them speak briefly then dismount. He was moving silently towards Brownell when Mose took the reins to both animals, leading them wearily towards the stable.

Brownell stood there a moment sizing up the rear of Caldwell's house. He punched his shirt deeper into his trousers, re-set the hat upon his head, lifted and re-settled the shell-belt and holstered six-gun upon his hip, then started softly forward towards the house. Jud let him get well clear of the stable-house before he moved speedily to intercept him. When he was athwart the big freighter's path he stepped into full view calling softly forward to the bearded man.

'Brownell!'

Instantly the large freighter froze. It appeared to take a moment for him to realise who was confronting him. Then his breath passed out in a long, low sigh. He did not move at all except to fling his dark gaze ahead to Jud. He seemed momentarily at a loss as to what course he should take. Then his shadowed face grew firmer; showed a decision. He was, as Jud saw, prepared to fight, but he was puzzled too, so stood entirely still. Very obviously he had expected nothing like this. He dropped his right hand to the vicinity of the holstered gun, then let it hang there. Jud was too close; Brownell recognised this and seemed to be thinking he had better raise that hand again, ball up the fist and use it as a guard. Jud was grinning at him, he appeared not in the least angry. He had both hands high along his great chest, each set of fingers curled and holding to the lapels of his coat. Then one hand flashed forward with blurring speed, caught Brownell on the side of the jaw and staggered him.

Brownell recovered, flung up both big fists and went forward in a driving lunge. Jud moved off stepping sideways. As the freighter's rusty beard loomed close Jud cocked and fired a powerful short jab. Brownell's booted feet became enmeshed; he went down and rolled over in the cinders. Jud was after him expecting Brownell to go for his gun. Brownell did, had the gun out and swinging when Jud's boot came down hard upon that hairy wrist, heel grinding into flesh. The big freighter's lips parted in a twisted grimace of agony. His fingers parted and Jud kicked the gun away then moved clear.

Brownell got up flexing his paining arm. There was murder in his expression now. He cat-footed forward then sprang, fingers like talons straining for Jud's coat, for something to grasp and hang on to, for this was the way Caleb Brownell fought; he was big and powerful, had never had to fight where he could not get his massive arms around an opponent and bearhug his victims senseless. But he was reacting instinctively now. He was not using his head at all, for Jud Parker was more than a physical match for the powerful freighter. He understood at once Brownell's intentions and did not step clear. Brownell's fingers caught and held; he swept Jud inward locking corded arms behind Parker's back. Jud had one arm free, his right one. He hesitated for Brownell's face to loom close, the freighter's shattered breathing to burst upon his cheeks, then he brought up that balled big fist and, getting a shoulder down behind the blow, stunned Brownell with a smashing blow between the eyes.

Claret sprayed, bones and cartilage splintered under Jud's fist and Brownell's arms dropped away. He let off a guttural cry from deep within him moving drunkenly clear with both hands over his face. Jud dug in his heels and followed; he hit the freighter a sinking blow in the middle, fist disappearing to the wrist. He caught him by one shoulder and half spun him away, then brought up a sledging punch that cracked with the sound of distant gunfire under Brownell's ear. The freighter's arms fell down hanging loose, he struggled to hold himself upright. Then very slowly, very leisurely, he slid down to flatten upon the cinder-path and Jud, holding his right fist in a cupped left hand, said a groaning curse. He had, he thought, broken a knuckle upon Brownell's skull. This irritated him because, having encountered that same granite head previously, he should have known better the second time.

He turned from the waist peering towards the stable-house. It was entirely silent and wholly dark. Evidently old Mose had heard nothing. Around front lamplight still shone outward from Heber Caldwell's study.

Jud drew in a great breath of refreshing night air, inspected his damaged hand, scooped up Brownell's pistol and tucked it carelessly into his trouser-top, then considered the sprawling form at his feet. With clinical detachment he thought that Caleb Brownell was a clumsy oaf; any Bowery tough in New York's tenderloin district could cut him to ribbons—providing Brownell was first disarmed. These legendary Westerners, he thought, bending to catch hold of the wrecked freighter, were over-rated. He picked Brownell off the ground as he'd have lifted a grain sack, then went along the side of Heber Caldwell's house to the front gallery and there let the big freighter fall with an echoing crash upon the porch floor. Using Brownell's pistol he struck the door twice, hard, bruising the wood, then, as he waited, he methodically punched out the gun's six loads, tossed them into the night behind him, and straightened his clothing.

Behind the door a waspish voice called cautiously: 'Who is it?'

'Brownell,' rumbled Jud.

The door swung inward, Heber Caldwell in his dressing gown stood thinly in the opening. ''Bout time you....'

Jud gravely viewed the old face with its swiftly altered expression at sight of him. He just as gravely held out Brownell's pistol butt-first. 'Here's your man,' he said, 'and here is his pistol. I told you, Caldwell. I warned you.'

Caldwell's eyes dropped to the swollen, face-up ruin at Jud's feet. Something like a whimper passed his lips.

'Take this gun,' ordered Jud.

But Caldwell stepped back crying. 'No; no you don't, Parker. You don't shoot me with a weapon in my hand.'

Jud held open his coat for Caldwell to see that he did not carry a sidearm. Then he flung the empty gun down at Caldwell's feet. 'Kill you?' he said, grimly smiling. 'That's the last thing I intend doing. You're valuable to me. I wouldn't kill you—unless you were stupid enough to try something like this again. But even then I wouldn't. Cripple you maybe, burn you out and break you down to size—but not kill you.'

71

Heber Caldwell started when a bubbling groan passed the lips of Caleb Brownell. 'He's not dead,' he blurted. And Jud, improvising on the spur of the moment, said to him, 'No, Mister Caldwell. My lads never kill 'em the first time.'

'Your lads. . . .'

'You're not as clever as I've heard,' said Jud, plunging both fisted hands deep into his trouser pockets. 'I'm not alone in this, Caldwell. I'm the leader and I do the fighting, but I'm not alone. I have eyes and ears all through Seward City. Guns too.' Jud prodded the unconscious freighter with one toe. 'Get a doctor for this one, Caldwell, and when he comes around give him a message for me. The next time I see him in Seward City I'll send a gunman to kill him. Tell him that, will you?'

'I'll tell him, Parker.'

Jud nodded. 'At the bank in the morning. Goodnight.'

He turned his back and strode away, ears straining for the cocking of Brownell's revolver, eyes alight with ironic amusement.

But Heber Caldwell made no move towards the gun; did not in fact even consider shooting Jud in the back, which he could not have accomplished with an empty gun anyway. Instead he stood there watching big Jud Parker fade out in the night, wearing an expression which showed respect, not fear, showing instead

72

of hatred, cold and understanding admiration. Then he lowered his glance as Jud's last footfalls atrophied, poked Brownell with his slippered foot and growled heartlessly.

'Lie there, you damned bungler!'

Slammed the door and disappeared deeper into his house.

CHAPTER EIGHT

It was nearly four o'clock in the morning when Jud Parker appeared silently behind the nighthawk at one of Seward City's liverybarns saying, 'I want a good tough horse and I want him right now.'

The night-man jumped, whirled about, gazed into big Jud Parker's rugged countenance, then hurried away saying, 'Yessir; right away, sir.'

He afterwards rode out of town heading north with a firm destination in mind, but with no actual directions on how to get there at hand. This, like all details, bothered him not one whit, and nearly two hours later, with the far-away eastern horizon brightening under the delicate pinkness of a fresh new day, he rode into the squalor of Buck Loring's Pothook Ranch. He'd asked the way only once, at a buffalo-hunter's soddy where a grizzled and filthy man had been firing up his breakfast cookery amid a pile of arranged stones twenty feet from his earthen home.

Loring's four riders were saddling horses when Jud appeared leisurely riding out of the morning's coolness. They studied him with frank curiosity. Three of them recognised him and nodded carefully as he went past heading for the log-and-mud house beyond where wispy smoke still half-heartedly rose from a battered stove-pipe chimney.

He dismounted, tied the livery beast and went to the front of Loring's home where he struck the door with his left fist—the unmarked, unswollen one. From within the house came first a strong epithet, then approaching bootsteps. Finally, the door swung inward and Buck stood there, unshaven, damp-eyed and obviously annoyed. At sight of big Jud, though, the rangeman's expression swiftly altered.

'What the devil,' he said. 'Come on in.'

Loring's darkly odorous residence was little better—certainly was no cleaner—than a Blackfeet lodge. It had the identical wild smells; a co-mingling of horsesweat, soiled leather and old cooking fat.

'I sure got smoked up last night,' said Loring, motioning Jud towards a stove which held, among other well-sooted implements, a battered old coffee pot. 'You eaten yet?'

'No,' said Jud candidly, eyeing the greasy plates and general filth. 'I'll eat later in town.'

74

He dropped into a chair as Buck Loring filled a tin mug with black coffee and began to drink it. 'You were well on the way last night when I saw you.'

'I got there,' groaned the rangeman, smacking his lips over the coffee. 'Man did I ever get there.' Loring suddenly recalled something; he turned to gaze with dawning respect upon Jud. 'How did you ever do it?'

'Do what?'

'Get to Mary Alice.'

Jud looked down at his injured hand, for a while saying nothing. Then he looked up again passing over Loring's question. 'I want you to fetch along your boys and ride into town with me,' he said. 'Right now.'

'Oh? You in some kind of trouble?'

'A little. Old Caldwell doesn't want to pay me some money he owes me.'

Buck said an obscene word, put down his cup and rummaged a shirt pocket for his tobacco sack. While he was shakily building his cigarette he began to frown. Finally he said, 'Wish I could oblige you, Jud, but me'n the boys got to go hunt some cattle today.'

'For a hundred dollars in addition to the fifty I owe you for the hay option?' murmured Jud.

Loring's damp gaze flung out over the half-formed cigarette. He then resumed his occupation, popped the cigarette into his mouth and lit it. On the exhale he said, 'For half that

75

much money I'd cheerfully put a bullet right 'tween old Heber's eyes.'

Jud leaned back in the chair gazing at the Texan. 'Seen Brownell lately?' he asked.

Buck repeated the same uncomplimentary word again and shook his head. 'His camp's still in my meadow though. Lex and Allie saw it yesterday.'

'Who are Lex and Allie?'

'Couple of my riders. They said Brownell's got his swampers armed for war, too.' Loring removed the cigarette, re-filled his coffee cup and sipped thoughtfully. 'Wish I had eight more good men. Damned if I wouldn't ride out there an' have a run at them.'

'How many of them are there?'

'Eleven, counting Brownell. Pretty hard crew, too. You got to be hard in that freighting business.'

Jud shifted position. 'I'll make you a bet,' he said. 'By the time you get back here from riding into Seward City with me, Brownell's wagons'll be gone from your range.'

Loring's quickening interest showed in his narrowing stare. He said, after a thoughtful moment, 'Jud; there's something about you I don't figure. You're a good man to drink with; you spend your money like a white man—but I keep gettin' a funny feelin' about you.' Loring finished his coffee, took a big drag off his cigarette, then continued speaking. 'For a

76

Yankee you're sort of unusual. 'Sure you didn't just say that; 'sure you aren't really a Texan?'

Jud got to his feet, genuinely smiling. 'We can talk on the trail. Get your lads and let's be riding.'

They left the house together. Loring called to his men telling them to fetch him a saddled horse, that they were not going to hunt cattle this day after all; they were going into town.

Later, as they loped overland southbound in the morning's clear brilliance, Jud drew in beside Loring to say, 'I don't want any trouble. No shooting. You boys just lounge around in front of the bank when I go in.'

'All right,' agreed Loring. 'How come old Caldwell to welch on you?'

'That's a long story. Maybe someday I'll tell you about it. Right now, you and your lads just stand around looking like you're going to start a war.'

'Maybe Caldwell'll start one.'

'Maybe. If he does I want him shot but not killed.'

Loring threw an amused look at Jud. 'Kind of a big order,' he said. 'When a man's in a spot he don't always aim like maybe he ought to.'

Jud nodded. 'Well; try not to kill the old devil anyway,' he said carelessly. 'In fact, don't start anythink at all, unless someone else opens up first.'

'I never do,' murmured Buck Loring, smiling

77

at Jud in an ironic way which hinted that this might not be altogether true.

They entered Seward City's bustle and turmoil all in a group, slowing their mounts at the very last moment in order to avoid the wagons, pedestrians, and light rigs which filled the roadway. It was still quite early but a thickening haze of heat was beginning to settle over the town; it mingled along Front Street with the pall of dun dust rising upwards from beneath steel tyres and shuffling horses' hooves.

Jud assumed full leadership, leading Loring's men to the liverybarn and there having them leave their animals. He also cleared a path through the tide of humanity which overflowed the roadside as far as Heber Caldwell's bank. There, with a significant glance at his rangemen companions, he left them to sweep on into the building.

The first person he encountered was Mary Alice Curry. She shot him a venomous look. Its intensity actually halted him in mid-stride. Then he smiled wickedly at her and resumed his way to the door beyond, with Heber Caldwell's name upon it. Without knocking he bored ahead past this partition and came face to face with the banker.

Caldwell was seated at a littered desk. He acknowledged Jud's entrance only by a lifting of his cold stare. An electric shock passed between these two men and the silence drew out to its

78

thinnest limit before Jud spoke.

'Sorry I'm a little late,' he said evenly. He had half expected Caldwell to have someone in the room with them, but they were quite alone. 'Have you the money?'

Caldwell gently eased back in his chair. Without speaking he raised a blue-veined hand to touch a thick envelope. Instead of answering he permitted this gesture to speak for him. Then he said, 'Parker; you're a young fool. I'm going to pay you. There'll be no trouble over that. But you're a fool.'

Jud scooped up the envelope, tore it open and fingered the bills it contained. He then pocketed the money and dropped the envelope upon Heber Caldwell's office floor.

'I can guess what your game is,' continued the banker, his calm poise thoroughly restored from the night before. 'And I can tell you that you'll never play it to its ending. Never, Parker.' Caldwell rocked forward and hooked his elbows upon the desk's edge staring unblinkingly upwards. 'You stumbled on to something yesterday. You were clever enough to capitalise on it. You got in a good stroke, Parker. You're a clever young man. Now be on your way. Try the Black Hills for gold. Try the galena mines or the silver pits. Don't stay in Seward City.'

Jud eased off in his stance, let all his massive weight rest upon one leg. He considered Caldwell's wizened face; read in its bloodless

79

gash of a mouth the greed of this older man; saw in Caldwell's dispassionate stare the carefully calculating ruthlessness, and smiled impudently down upon old Heber.

'My daddy died when I was six,' he said to Caldwell. 'My mother ran off when I was seven. Ever since then I've been playing odds, Caldwell. Do you know the kind of odds I mean?'

'I think I know them, yes. Only Parker—I've been playing the same odds a lot longer. About forty years longer, and they're no longer odds to me. They're the facts of life and I know them forwards and backwards. Like I said: You'll never win in this game.'

Jud's smile grew flinty. He thought that this old man was the fool; all old men were who had amassed such wealth. They were stationary targets. They could manoeuvre only within a prescribed radius, always vulnerable because around them lay the substance of their power, their wealth, while he, Jud Parker, had the initiative. He could manoeuvre any way he chose because, succinctly, he had everything to gain and nothing to lose. He continued to smile down into that coldly calculating face.

'I like your advice,' he said. 'If I'd had a father who told me these things I probably would have listened to him.' Jud went as far as the door and there faced back around. 'One more thing: did you give Brownell my message?'

80

'I did.'

'Will he obey it?'

'How would I know. Caleb's a hard, rough man.'

'You'd know because he's also *your* man.'

'All right; he'll probably do as you said. But I can't guarantee it.'

'You'd better guarantee it,' said Jud, almost amiably. 'Because if his wagons are still up there in Loring's pasture this evening I'm going to visit you again, and this time I'll pull your fine white house down around your ears stick by stick.'

He left the office with Heber Caldwell's warming glare fixed upon his wide shoulders. Afterwards, old Heber summoned a clerk and irritably snapped at him: 'Get a horse; ride to Brownell's camp and tell him to pull out with the freight he already has. Tell him to go on over to Custer and deliver it. If he argues with you about not having a pay-load, tell him I said for him to roll out and right now—this morning.'

Jud, savouring his first victory in this raw land he was determined to conquer, pushed through the crowd in Caldwell's vault-like outer space and again encountered Mary Alice. She had, he felt, been waiting for him to return. She drew him aside with her smouldering, commanding stare, and when he was close hissed at him.

'You're despicable; I loathe men like you!'

81

'The difference between me and old Caldwell,' he told her quietly, 'is that I don't dream of what I'd have done to you thirty years ago. I'll do it right now—in this damned crowded bank, if I feel like it.'

She blanched, completely frightened of him for the first time because she saw in his bold face the truth of what he said. She started to move swiftly away but he caught an arm whirling her back towards him. 'Give me time,' he said. 'I'll give you what you want out of life. I swear that to you. Just give me time.' He let her go adding to this. 'Six o'clock this evening—supper at the hotel.'

'No,' she flared at him. 'Even if I wanted to a dozen people would see us. *He* would find out. Don't you realise he'd give a thousand dollars to know how you worked that hay deal on him?'

'All right; not the hotel then. I'll pick you up in a top-buggy and we'll just go driving. No one'll see you then.'

'I wouldn't,' she flared at him, 'go driving with you if you were the last man on earth!'

'Then maybe I'd better remind you right now with another kiss that I'm not the last man on earth.'

She took a rapid backwards step gazing up at him in horror. 'No! All these people. . . .'

'Six o'clock, then?'

He was cruelly smiling at her.

'Yes. All right. Only please go now.'

He turned upon his heel and passed out into the yonder roadway, sighted Buck Loring, moved forward towards the rangeman with one big hand reaching inside his coat.

Under Loring's wide eyes Jud counted out one hundred and fifty dollars and passed them over. Then he gazed over Loring's head thinking, and finally he said, 'I'll give you the money for the others if you'll take it to them for me.'

'Sure,' said Loring, counting his money laboriously, each feature of his sun-darkened face still mirroring disbelief. 'Sure; any way you want to do it.'

Jud also counted out and handed over this other money, then he looped his arm under Loring's elbow saying, 'Let's get a drink. All this talking makes my throat burn.'

The five of them, Jud, Buck Loring, and Loring's riders, stepped down into the roadway dust making for the Warbonnet Saloon. With the exception of Jud Parker they were each of them thinking only of this particular moment. Jud was thinking of something less pleasant: When Loring discovered the hay he was going to put up now belonged to his hated enemy, Heber Caldwell, Jud might not only lose his only friend in Seward City; he might even find the Texan's wrath—and his gun—hard to ameliorate.

Well; when one made big profits, he thought

calmly, one had also to accept the responsibilities and perils they engendered. When the time came, or before, he'd find a way around Buck Loring. He had to; he had another plan in mind and this one, he was sure, would require guns. He was not finished with Heber Caldwell yet—not by a long sight.

CHAPTER NINE

The day was well along towards afternoon when Jud Parker left Loring, went to his dingy room, flung his possessions into his only carpetbag and returned to the Seward City Hotel. There, because cheaper rooms were unavailable—and also because he felt expansive—he paid for a suite, called for bath water to be brought up, sent for the tailor who had been unable to adequately patch his coat, ordered a steak dinner sent up, and climbed heavily to his new quarters.

He was tired, his side ached from the long horseback ride, he needed a shave, but he felt better than he'd felt in a long time. When the meal came he ate prodigiously, sent the boy back for a box of cigars, then bathed. Was still bathing when the tailor arrived. He shouted through the door that he wanted a new Prince Albert coat, new trousers, and new linen, and he wanted them at once. The tailor departed, beaming. He rarely got such excellent assignations against his stock of quality ready-made clothing; usually his trade was limited to the selling of cowhide boots, flannel shirts and woollen trousers. He joined the crowded multitudes of people in the roadway whose haste did not now exceed the tailor's own haste.

Jud was sprawled titan-like upon the bed when the tailor returned burdened with garments. He sat up, lit a cigar under the tailor's admiring stare, then stood up bare to the hips. Here, thought the tailor, was a man to match the mountains; his enormous trunk rippled with flat muscles, each one moving smoothly under a tight, glowingly healthy hide. There was something definitely primitive about this powerful Jud Parker, he thought, something quite splendidly masculine. He bent to quickly hold up his best garments for Jud to try, and with each selection Jud made the tailor privately as well as outwardly agreed. When the last choice hd been made Jud stood toweringly magnificent. He had the physique for clothing; that bizarre quality some men possessed to make whatever he wore appear to be the best possible quality. He paid the tailor from a great roll of bills and sent him off, then very carefully put aside the clothing, eased down again upon the bed and, turning upon his side, slept like a babe until lengthening shadows warned him of the approaching hour of his engagement with Mary Alice Curry.

He re-dressed, this time more carefully, combed back that great shock of glinting hair that covered his head, examined himself in a mirror, smiled without warmth, with calculating coolness at his reflection, then passed out of the room, down the hotel stairway and passed along out into the lowering dusk of early evening.

At the liverybarn he secured a new top-buggy with isinglass curtains that crinkled and drove leisurely to Mary Alice's home. He could, by whipping up the horse, have arrived there on time, but he did not do this. And when he alighted, dropped the tether-weight then pushed forward towards the door of this small, neat house, he was not even thinking about Mary Alice Curry at all. He was very carefully smoothing the edges of a plan he'd been considering on and off since early morning; since that long and lonely ride out to Loring's Pothook Ranch.

The door swung back revealing Mary Alice beyond its threshold. She looked into his face, then very slowly lowered her glance and swept it back up him again. 'Come in,' she said in a totally neutral tone. 'I've changed my mind. I'm not going riding with you.'

He passed on into the neat, attractive parlour, gazed boldly around it with approval, then faced her.

86

'You coerced me anyway. You know that—threatening me at the bank this morning.'

He said: 'I wasn't threatening you. I was making you a promise.'

'Yes. In front of all those people—I think you would have kept it, too.'

'What makes you think I won't keep it now—here?'

'Because you have no audience,' she murmured, moving past him, seating herself near a window beyond which the descending night was puddling. She glanced up at him, saw him grow cold, grow keen, with the identical resolve he'd shown her at the bank. She bit her lip; she'd made a bad mistake. He *would* do it here. He wasn't, as she'd thought in a moment of angry bad judgment, at the bank, the kind of a man who did everything for effect. He wasn't that kind at all. He was simply beyond prediction. She looked swiftly away saying, 'Please sit down. How angry do you think Mister Caldwell was; can you imagine?'

'Fit to be tied,' he said.

'Did he pay you?'

'Didn't he tell you he was going to?' he countered. 'You're his right arm.'

She murmured, 'Yes; he told me he was going to.' Then she met his gaze head-on as she'd done before with that same hard earnestness. 'I'm going to tell you why he paid you.'

'Do that, Mary Alice,' he said softly. 'Do that.'

Her gaze hardened still more; it was readable in her face that she wanted to hurt him, to baffle him. To rake his armour of confidence with figurative fingernails.

'He told you that you were a fool, didn't he?'

Jud nodded, watching her beautiful face which all the bitterness could not mar. 'He did.'

'And you thought he meant because you'd hurled yourself at him like that—with threats and violence.'

'What else did he mean?'

'That you really *are* a fool, Jud. He didn't have to buy those options at all. If all he wanted was to force up the winter price of hay he had only to over-bid your options and fight you with his wealth.'

Jud's eyes grew still and intently watchful. Even his tone altered away from its former heartiness. Within him was stirring an uneasiness. 'Go on,' he told her. 'Get to the point.'

'I didn't tell you the whole story last night. I would have, I suppose, the way I was feeling then. But I didn't.'

'Get on with it, dammit.'

'He hadn't even approached the hay growers. Didn't that make you even a little bit suspicious?'

'No. Why should it have? He hadn't had time yet.'

Mary Alice smiled cruelly. 'You *are* a fool, Jud. Men like Heber Caldwell move swiftly once they are ready to move. He hadn't gone to the hay growers because he only completed his contracts with the Army yesterday afternoon. *Jud; he contracted that five hundred tons of stacked hay to the Quartermaster Corps at forty-five dollars a ton!*'

Jud's face darkened with the swift rush of hot blood. Over twenty thousand dollars—and he'd settled for a quarter as much!

Mary Alice, seeing his swelling fury and humiliation, laughed.

He looked out the window beyond her. Twilight had passed now, giving way to darkness. His furious stare ran on to the dim-merging outlines of trees standing against this paler darkness. Then, very gradually, he began to smile. There was no warmth or genuine amusement in this slow-coming smile, there was chagrin.

'I *was* a fool,' he told her. Then he laughed too, keeping from her the secret which amused him. Sure, old Heber had made a killing with the options, but he could have afforded to. Jud's comparatively small profit must indeed look insignificant beside Caldwell's killing—but he'd had exactly sixty-six dollars in the world when he'd obtained the options; relatively, he'd netted as much as Heber had and this meant to him that he was still as wily as old Heber. It meant something else as well, to him; he was Caldwell's match; he wanted to pair-up dollars with old Heber again to see who really was the fool. He meant right now to implement this so he chuckled, continuing to look chagrined, until he saw Mary Alice's tawny eyes soften towards him. Then he stopped laughing to speak to her.

'Do you know, Mary Alice—I don't really mind. Not really. Would you like to know why?'

'Yes,' she said, then her gaze widened, darkened, became suddenly no longer poised nor cruel not even commanding as he arose from his chair and crossed to stand before her in three huge strides.

'Because,' he exclaimed in a deep-timbred tone, holding her gaze easily with his stare. 'Because, while he has his money I've got something he wants the worst way and can never have. Never, never, never. *You!*'

She seemed to draw back in her chair. 'Please,' she murmured to him. 'Go back. Please, Jud—sit down.'

He reached down to draw her up out of the chair. He had upon his face that peculiar, triumphant look again, that challenging, demanding brittle smile he'd worn after the last time she'd been in his arms. He held her close, so close in the steel band of his arms that her body pressing the length of him gouged into his

90

sore right side. He enjoyed this slight pain. Against the brutal strength of his arms she was powerless. He bent low seeking lips. They were there, not avoiding him this time, but cold to his touch as before, bitter, tight-closed and unresponsive. He let his want sear her mouth, hurt it. Through the thick dark forest of partially closed lashes he watched for, and saw, lines of pain appear up around her own pinched-closed lids.

Now he changed to gentleness. Then her response, as before, was there. Her face moving beneath his, her great wealth of coppery hair tumbling over his fore-arm, her beautiful, mature features colouring with a tumult of rushing blood. Her lips caught at him, holding him; they parted under his pressure. Her arms swept upwards along his great shoulders digging at the great-corded muscles there, kneading them. She gasped his name, moaned it.

He stepped clear.

She staggered, caught herself and flung him a terrible look with rising tears scalding her eyes, filling them with blurring speed.

'Jud. Oh, Jud. . .!'

He drew her along towards a little sofa and let her down there. He was, behind the impassivity of his handsome, cruel and rugged face, laughing silently at her.

Still with her hand in his fingers he removed his Prince Albert, cast it carelessly upon a table and then knelt at her side saying, 'Do you still think I just might be that man, Mary Alice; that man you said I couldn't be in a thousand years?'

'Yes,' she whispered, touching his face, entirely changed from the haughty woman he'd first noticed at the Seward City hotel's dining-room. 'Oh yes, Jud.'

He smiled, a wintry smile, took her hand and kissed it with his bowed head and its mass of thick hair neatly in her lap. Then he moved easily from under her free hand where it was moving through his hair, saying, 'Old Caldwell's got a rival, Mary Alice.'

'No,' she murmured to him, seeking in the boldness of his face something hoped for. 'Mister Caldwell ceased to exist for me night before last, Jud. He never in this world could be your rival. Never.'

He put forth a hand and let it rest upon her throat, in his palm a sturdy pulse slammed unevenly. Her flesh was hot to the touch.

'He's my rival all right, Mary Alice. He made a fool of me today.'

'He'll never do that again, Jud. I promise you.

'Jud. . .?'

'Yes.'

'Kiss me. Love me. . . .'

He straightened up to lean towards her. Beyond this room night-shadows dripped their formless substance into the long, long hours that passed.

CHAPTER TEN

Lying in bed at the Seward City hotel with summer sunlight gradually filling his room, Jud Parker thought of something he'd heard often enough in his lifetime: Something to the effect that women were the worst gossips under the sun.

He had known enough women to know they couldn't hold a candle to men for pure gossip. But he had also known enough women to know something else which might have originally inspired that perverted axiom, and that was simply that an infatuated woman would say anything she was asked to say while in the passionate embrace of a lover.

It had been so ridiculously easy. Mary Alice's veneer had disappeared in a twinkling, if indeed she'd ever really been as sophisticated as Jud had originally thought her. Right now, lying there all loose and languid with only his mind carrying him forward into the new day, he thought that Mary Alice Curry was different from Sharon Caldwell in only one respect; Mary Alice *knew*—she was a full woman with a full woman's fire and certain knowledge. She was no tremulous girl. He threw back the coverlets saying aloud in a voice like distant spring-thunder: 'Thank God for that.' And he meant it because big Jud Parker was an impatient man, ambition was driving him, the profit he'd made on the hay-options had banked new fires in his heart. He wanted no tender petal to crush, he wanted no quivering passion which would burst its floodgates and inundate him, possess him, stifle him, drown him. He wanted a balanced, full woman. He swung his legs to the floor and shot upright—then hung there, astonished at his own searing thoughts. *He wanted Mary Alice Curry!*

No, he silently roared at himself in rebuke. No, no, no. There was no place in his life for a wife. Well; not yet anyway. Then he relaxed and bitterly smiled. Besides she'd hate him all over again after last night. She'd despise him because she'd know this morning what she'd told him of Caldwell's secret affairs and she'd know absolutely that again he'd used her, and furthermore that he had done that deliberately so that he could have a second advantage over her employer.

She might even run to the old man and tell him. No, she wouldn't do that. She loathed Heber Caldwell. He reached for his trousers, stepped into them and kicked into his boots. He went to the window and gazed outward and downward. Seward City was alive with shoppers, with the usual early-day wagon and buggy traffic. He raised a huge arm and scratched his head.

But she just might try thwarting him. She was capable enough of that, was tawny-eyed Mary Alice Curry with her running-deep, her running-strong, unsuspected passion. He finished dressing and left the room bound for the dining-room. It was one of his idiosyncrasies that when he'd been roistering he was invariably afterwards voraciously hungry. He now moved solidly to satisfy that hunger before moving on to what must be done this day.

He noticed for the first time since his arrival in Seward City that the people, commencing with the waiters at breakfast, knew who he was. It was a good sensation, being deferred to. It made him a little heady. He was rising slowly and did not immediately see the tall young man approaching. Did not notice the fine-etched features nor the athletic grace of this youthful stranger. Then the young man halted, speaking softly to Jud.

'Mister Parker; they pointed you out to me.'

Jud looked up. Considered the smoke-grey, steady eyes which were on a level with his own eyes. Saw the way he was coolly being measured, weighed, assessed. He nodded, waiting. This young man made him feel oversized and massively awkward. He was as tall as Jud but was more finely made; he was erect yet had the appearance of being entirely loose

95

and at ease.

'Mister Parker I want to work for you.'

Jud blinked. 'Work for me—how? I have no store, no. . . .'

'Any way you can use me. I heard from Sharon Caldwell what you did to her father.'

Jud's brows climbed slightly, his bold eyes hardened a little. He began to wonder if Sharon Caldwell meant anything to this tall stranger; he also wondered if Sharon had said what Jud had also done to her. Softly, rumblingly he said, 'Go on.'

'He had me run out of Seward City last year, Mister Parker. Had me beaten up, put on a stage and taken out of the county.'

'I see,' murmured Jud, beginning to understand. 'What's your name?'

'Albert Millam, sir.'

'Al? Do they call you Al?'

'They call me Bert.'

'Well, Bert; why did Caldwell have you whipped and run off?'

'I wanted to marry Sharon.'

'And. . .?'

'She was willing to marry me too.'

'You weren't good enough?'

'That's correct, sir.'

Jud cleared his throat. He viewed the young man flintily. 'Quit calling me "sir",' he growled. 'Come along; I've got to go over to the liverybarn.'

They left the dining-room together, Jud massively swaying, Bert Millam a lean shadow at his side. Outside there was a bright sun burning; spring was past and from here on there would be lassitude-producing heat. Jud halted, very carefully turning several thoughts over in his mind. Millam stood silently, patiently waiting. Jud said, 'All right; I'll try you.' He peered from under dark brows at Millam, 'But I might as well tell you that I don't trust strangers. Not now—not here in Caldwell's town.'

Millam said quietly, 'If I thought you did, Mister Parker, I wouldn't work for you.'

Jud's eyes widened, held to Millam's handsome face a moment, then twinkled with gradual amusement. He laughed aloud saying, 'Maybe I need someone like you at that, Bert. Tell me—what is it exactly that you want in life?'

'Sharon Caldwell, Mister Parker, then a lot of money. I want them in that order.'

Jud nodded. He said, growling again, 'Stop calling me "Mister Parker." Call me Jud.'

'Yes—Jud.'

'Where are you from, Bert?'

'New York—Jud.'

'The hell. Well; I like that. Who are your folks?'

'I am alone. I came to the Dakotas because I heard tall tales of gold and good land and
97

opportunities.'

Jud's bold stare kindled to a warmness. Millam was very young, perhaps no more than twenty, but he had that essential confidence successful men had to have. What he evidently lacked was experience. Jud's wide mouth curled slightly upwards. Well; young Millam could gain experience working for him—it might not be the kind of experience mothers wished for their sons to acquire but by God it was worthwhile experience.

He said: 'You know the countryside, do you, Bert?'

'Passably well, yes.'

'Then let's get you a livery horse and you ride out to Buck Loring's Pothook Ranch and tell Loring I want to see him this afternoon. Can you do that?'

'Yes, sir. Excuse me: Yes, Jud.'

They got the animal and Jud watched young Bert Millam lope gracefully north out of town. He then bit the end off his first cigar of the day, lit it, and walked sturdily down to the Seward City Bank. There, making his way steadily through the bedlam and press of swarming miners, merchants, freighters and others seeking to deposit or withdraw money, he passed around the rough front counter's far right curving and loomed up before the discreetly located small desk of Mary Alice Curry. She saw him immediately and moved

98

only to put aside the pen in her hand, lift her deeply calm, deeply inscrutable face, and meet his down-sweeping gaze with a look that was limpid.

As was his custom, when something was heavily upon his mind, he ignored the amenities saying to her, 'Why doesn't Sharon shoot that old devil?'

'What?'

'I met a young buck named Millam. Old Caldwell ran him off because he wasn't good enough for his daughter.'

'Oh,' murmured Mary Alice. 'That was last year. It was foolish of him to return to town. Mister Caldwell will hear of it. He won't like it at all.'

Mary Alice was saying things by rote; her voice was without inflection, without depth or timbre. She was watching his face with her full attention; the kind of full attention which could come only from deep interest, strong longing.

'Maybe,' rumbled Jud. 'Maybe he shouldn't have come back. Then again, maybe he should have.'

'Jud . . .?'

'Yes.'

'What are you thinking?'

He smiled that slow, hard smile at her. He bent slightly and lay a hand lightly upon her, then straightened away saying, 'Never mind that, Mary Alice. I've got something special to say to you—but not yet. Business comes first.'

She said in a near-whisper, a knowing look upon her face. 'He'll kill you, Jud. This time he'll have you killed. Please—for my sake, if you care at all for me—please don't go against him again.'

He rocked slightly upon his toes gazing steadily upon her. God, she was a fine looking woman, high-breasted, round-hipped with eyes that changed shades with her moods, and her face was a mask that hid away the banked fires of her. It was a beautiful face, too. 'Tell you what,' he said thickly. 'Do you know Sharon Caldwell very well?'

'Well enough I suppose. What is it you want with her?'

'Have her at your house this evening. Can you manage that?'

'I think so. Jud . . .?'

But he was already moving away, his eyes brightly scheming, his great stride carrying him along through the crowd until she lost even his towering head and shoulders at the doorway.

Beyond, in the burning sunlight, Jud came abruptly face to face with a man whose immediate impact upon him was entirely unexpected. Caleb Brownell.

He saw at once that his own appearance had the identical effect upon the big, bearded freighter. Brownell stiffened his full length, staring out of unwavering small eyes.

100

'You don't remember so good,' said Jud. 'Do you?'

'I remember all right, Mister Parker,' rumbled the freighter. 'And I'm here a-purpose to see you.'

Jud threw outward his flickering gaze to encompass Brownell. He said, 'All right. Step around behind the building with me.'

'No,' Brownell got off quickly, 'it's not for that I was lookin' for you.'

'What then?'

'Folks are talkin' about your feud with old Heber. That's what I'd like to talk to you about.'

'Talk,' commanded Jud, standing there wide-legged so that the pedestrian traffic broke around him. 'You're his man—so talk.'

'That's just it, Mister Parker, I ain't Caldwell's man. He's got my wagons and teams bound to him by mortgages, but I ain't his man. He makes me do his dirty work, like he makes a lot of other folks who're bounden to him—but I'm all through. He can have the wagons—I'm quitting. A man can take just so much, then he's either got to sell his self-respect or get out. Me, I'm gettin' out.'

'You said all that to tell me what?' queried Jud Parker.

'Heber's got my freight line lock stock an' barrel. I've built up my business until it's the biggest and best in the Territory, but he's got it in his pocket with those damned mortgages. I make good money—it nearly all goes to him. But, Mister Parker—he needs my line. I do all the heavy freighting. Move all the heavy stuff like mining machinery, stamp mills, big lots of groceries. Without my line the local commerce would be hard hit; the other little one-rig outfits hereabouts couldn't begin to handle the heavy shipments.'

'Get to the point, Brownell.'

'All right; I heard a rumour he's going to foreclose and clean me out—then run the business himself.'

'How does that concern me?'

'I need a thousand dollars cash to hold him off.'

'Then get it, Brownell. I'm not a freighter.'

'I can't get it, Mister Parker. No one but you is willing to buck old Heber. I couldn't get a thin dime, if folks knew I figured to use it in a fight with Heber. Folks are too scairt of him; he owns most of 'em anyway.'

Jud gazed upon Caleb Brownell for a long, thoughtful moment, then he said, 'Come on over to my hotel room,' and turned upon his heel.

Brownell clumped along after Jud, entered the hotel at his side, went upstairs to Jud's room, and did not emerge for a full hour, but when he eventually did, he was grimly smiling for in his pocket was a crumpled roll of large bills; a thousand dollars in cash.

CHAPTER ELEVEN

Jud was carefully dressing when Bert Millam
came softly knocking on his door. He called for
Millam to enter and went on dressing, his back
to the youth.

'I got him,' reported Bert. 'He'll be along in a
little while.'

Jud said nothing. He was struggling with the
elusive froth of a handsome silk cravat. With a
crashing oath he tore the thing off and wheeled
about. 'One thing about being poor,' he snarled.
'You don't have to put up with these
confounded things.'

Millam moved closer, took the cravat and
deftly tied it on Jud. Then he stepped away
thinly smiling, saying nothing. Jud faced
around again, viewed himself in a mirror and
said, 'Thanks.' He patted the cravat. 'Bert; how
long you been back in Seward City?'

'Only today. I arrived on the morning stage.'

'And right away you heard about me?'

'Yes, they told me at the Marshal's office.'

Jud faced around, brows down darkly. 'What
were you doing at the Marshal's office?'

Millam opened his coat to reveal beneath it a
belted pistol on a bullet-studded shell-belt.

'There's an ordinance in Seward City—if you carry sidearms you're supposed to register them with the Marshal. That's another of Caldwell's regulations.' Millam let the coat close, hiding his armament again.

Jud's frown deepened. 'Do you know how to use that thing?'

'Yes sir. Passably well.'

Jud began to negatively shake his head. 'Take it off,' he ordered. 'Passably well isn't good enough, boy. When a man starts settling his troubles with guns he's got to be the absolute best. Being passably good will only get you killed.'

He waited for Bert Millam to obey but the tall, lithe youth made no move to do so. He almost languidly moved his right arm forward, then started bringing it back along his right side to sweep away the coat. Jud, watching, did not see the gun come out at all; he simply saw its ugly black snout tilted toward his face. He looked slowly from the weapon to Bert Millam's thinly smiling eyes. Then he sighed, reached for his coat upon the bed, shrugged into it and growled. 'Where did you learn to draw a gun like that?'

'In New Mexico Territory, sir,' said Millam. 'I spent a year down there.' Bert's smiling mouth was mocking. 'Shall I take it off, now?'

'No,' growled Jud. 'Only next time tell the truth—you're not passably good with that

104

thing—you're lightning-fast.' He passed along as far as the door, then halted. 'Come along. Sharon's waiting for you. But first we'll have a little supper.'

In the dining-room people entered and left, frequently throwing guardedly interested glances upon Jud. Occasionally someone would nod and Jud nodded back. He relished this meal as he had the earlier one, but in the back of his calculating mind he was not fooled; he had triumphed, yes, but it had not netted him a tenth as much as these people evidently thought it had. Or maybe that wasn't it at all; maybe it was simply that their lively interest was piqued by the fact that Jud had dared cross old Caldwell. By the time he settled back to light a cigar, he thought this was plausibly what intrigued the people of Seward City. He exhaled, cleared his mind of these thoughts and bent a long stare upon young Millam, who had scarcely touched his meal, and whose clear, observing eyes were now quite lively, quite shiny.

It required no vast powers of understanding to divine what was passing in Millam's mind and Jud removed the cigar to say gruffly, 'I expect you know the old man'll eat you alive.'

'Perhaps,' murmured Millam. 'But he might choke on a bone this time.' Millam brushed his right hand over the low bulge beneath his coat. 'Last time I was a stranger—I didn't know how

Caldwell operated.'

'It helps,' Jud commented drily, 'to know your opponent.' He arose, mouthed his cigar and gazed beyond the window where dusk was settling. 'Always take your time. Rush into nothing. People have patterns. Learn them before you get to know the people. It saves time and sometimes it also saves lives. Let's go.'

They could easily have walked the short distance to Mary Alice Curry's house but Jud preferred riding so they rented a rig and drove there.

Jud was thoughtful and entirely silent until they drew up. Then he did not at once alight. Instead, looping the lines, he said, 'Something else, Bert: When you hit a man hit him with everything you've got—swamp him—bowl him over. Never give him a chance to recover from your attack. Keep him off balance and reeling.' He turned to gaze upon Millam. 'Don't talk. Talking men are not fighters and fighting men don't talk. That applies to lovers too. You remember that.'

'I will, sir.'

Jud moved to get down. He growled, 'Damn it, I told you to quit calling me "sir."'

'I'm sorry.'

Jud paused across the horse. He watched Millam move gracefully clear of the rig. He sighed; if he'd had a younger brother he'd have wished for him to have Millam's poise, his easy

106

manners, his quiet, cold confidence.

Then he started forward.

Where they came together at the narrow approach to Mary Alice Curry's residence he said to Millam: 'Sharon's supposed to be here.'

Millam faltered in his stride, but only very briefly. 'Isn't this where old Caldwell's secretary lives?'

'It is. What of it?'

'Well; nothing.'

'Say it—what of it?'

'I've heard it said she's as ice-cold as old Caldwell himself is.'

'That,' said Jud, 'was last year.' He halted, raised a huge fist, and lightly struck the door.

Mary Alice admitted them. She scarcely saw Bert Millam at all. Moving past for them to enter she said softly to Jud, 'She's here.'

Jud had seen Sharon. She had also seen him where she stood in the parlour and her face went white at the sight of him. He stepped away saying gruffly to Bert, and avoiding Sharon's eyes, 'Go on; Mary Alice and I'll be outside on the porch.'

But Mary Alice took Jud's arm and led him along into the yonder pantry. There she sat down at a table motioning for him to do likewise.

'That won't make you any money,' she said.

He dropped down, understanding what she meant, and he shrugged. 'It doesn't have to.' He looked across at her, his eyes sweeping boldly across that slight and intervening distance. 'Not directly, anyway. He loves her.'

'You're not that warm-hearted, Jud. Not you. Another man might be—but not you. You're ruthless; why did you do it?'

'I want him to marry her.'

'Again—why?'

He stirred; annoyance kindled behind his lashes. 'You ask an awful lot of questions, Mary Alice,' he growled, then switched the conversation. 'Why does Caldwell want to break Caleb Brownell?'

She continued to sit there studying him. Then she said, 'Jud, you only use people. In the end I think you ruin them—and enjoy doing it.'

He put a big scarred hand upon the table, drummed lightly with it.

'I'm so ashamed of myself I could cry, Jud.'

His rough voice said rumblingly, 'For last night? You shouldn't be, Mary Alice.' He paused, drew back a big breath, then speaking swiftly, said to her, 'I want you. I want to marry you. If anyone had told me a week ago I'd be saying this I'd have laughed in his face.'

She very gently shook her head at him. She saw him now through a quickening mist. 'I'm something to be used. Don't make it worse. You don't want to marry me, you only want to keep me dangling until you've gotten all the information from me you can; information that will help you fight Mister Caldwell.'

His drumming fingers slowly curled into a fist. He struck the table making it jump under impact. 'Damn Caldwell,' he grated. 'I know all I have to know to fight him. Leave him out of this. *I want to marry you!*'

She was shaken; he could see this and it heightened his longing. Then she had control again; her eyes became quite dry, quite hard and calculating. In almost a whisper she said, 'All right, Jud; you're going to have a chance to keep your word.' She arose swiftly to stand above him looking hotly into his face. 'I'll marry you tonight—right now. I'll send young Millam for the minister.'

He sat there, bit fist loosening, bold eyes darkening, drawing away from her bitter intensity. She had called him, had flung down the challenge for him to accept or sidestep. He looked away from her with colour mounting into his face. But it was not an expression she correctly interpreted he was angered by her fierce and commanding manner, not by what she had said.

His gaze went back to her face, saw its slow paling, its gradual, terrible and bitter disillusionment, and he also arose. 'Send for him,' he snarled at her. 'Get a dozen damned preachers if it'll make you happy. I meant every lousy word I said.'

She dropped like stone back into the chair,

lay her face upon both arms and broke into wild
sobbings. Jud's flaring nostrils and reddened
face became bewildered. He hung there
unmoving, unsure of himself, then he drew
away, went to the parlour and said to Bert
Millam: 'Go to the Warbonnet and find Buck
Loring. Tell him I want to see him here. Then
round up a preacher and fetch him back with
you too.'

At Millam's slack-jawed look Jud's flush
deepened and he muttered unpleasantly, 'Well;
don't stand there. Go on!'

Millam left at once.

For several moments Jud stood in the parlour
saying nothing, then, when the door closed after
Millam, he roused himself to cast a hostile stare
at Heber Caldwell's daughter. There was a
fascinated look in Sharon's unblinking stare.
She might, he thought, be looking upon a
rattlesnake instead of Jud Parker. He forced his
voice to soften when he addressed her now.

'He wants to marry you. He came back here
just for that. Your paw had him beaten last year
an' he's taking a big chance in being in your
paw's town right now.'

She said so softly that he scarcely heard her: 'I
know.'

'Well; he said you wanted to marry him last
year. What I want to know is whether or not you
still want to?'

'Yes. Oh yes, I *do* want to. But my

father. . . .'

Jud spoke a hard oath. 'Tonight your father's going to have his nice drink of good wine in the expensive security of his big white-painted house, girl. He might as well be a million miles away. Tonight—for once in your life—show some of the spirit you must have inherited from him. Do as you like—make up your own mind.'

Sharon stood tall and willowy and fully silent, her face white from throat to temple, her troubled gaze fixed hypnotically upon big Jud Parker. She murmured, 'We'll have to leave Seward City, Mister Parker.'

'Then leave it,' he boomed at her, his patience shattering. 'When a man loves a woman he'll make sacrifices. Does it only work one way, girl?'

'No. Oh no, Mister Parker.'

He wheeled away leaving Sharon Caldwell to sink weakly upon a settee with lace antimacassars upon its back and arm-rests; stormed back into the pantry—and almost collided with Mary Alice Curry whose dried eyes and scarlet lips caught and held his hot attention.

She said: 'What sacrifice would *you* make, Jud?'

'Name it,' he commanded her. 'Name it and by God I'll make it.'

'All right, Jud. Tell me in three words why you want to marry me. And if you choose the right words you know what you'll be sacrificing—your freedom.'

He said stormily, 'I love you.'

She fell into his iron embrace, her last doubt stilled.

CHAPTER TWELVE

There was an air of unreality about those two marriages, accomplished in a stilted double ceremony by a minister whose trepidation after he saw whom he was to seal in matrimony, left him badly shaken and breathless for almost the entire length of time it took to complete his duty.

Except for the blinding brightness of big Jud Parker's compelling stare he probably would not have performed the ceremony for Sharon Caldwell and Bert Millam at all, for he was primarily a cautious man, and he could visualise with no effort at all Heber Caldwell's fury at his daughter's marriage—as well as venomous old Heber's instantaneous reaction.

On the other hand Heber Caldwell's dreaded personality was absent from the household of Mary Alice Curry while the majestically imposing great bulk of this man, Jud Parker, was very much in evidence, and the minister, as well as everyone else in Seward City, knew by this time that Parker was, if anything—because he was much younger, much larger physically and therefore physically dangerous—just as bad a man to cross as Caldwell was.

He was in such a hurry to depart after the double marriage ceremony that only Jud's roar halted him at the door. Jud went forward, pressed a number of bills into the reverend's hand, then held the door for, and closed it after, his nearly running feet, and leaned upon it gazing at—Mrs. Judson Parker.

Buck Loring, who had served as a very solemn and not altogether reconciled witness, sank heavily on to a chair gazing from one face to another. Then he rubbed his jaw and squinted ahead at Jud saying quietly, 'I got a feeling the lot of us are going to think the blinking sky fell in on us when old Heber hears about this.'

Jud swung his probing gaze from Buck to Mary Alice. He lifted his great shoulders and let them fall; he was very faintly smiling. 'Let it fall,' he breathed, holding Mary Alice stationary with his stare. 'I sure could use some strong black coffee—Mrs. Parker. From the looks of them I'm sure Buck and Bert could too.'

Mary Alice nodded. She turned a little stiffly, caught at Sharon's hand murmuring something to the younger girl. They passed together out of the parlour.

'You're not the type,' mused Loring aloud to

Jud. 'It's hard to believe you actually did it.'

'You were a witness,' said Jud in reply, then swung the talk to what was in his mind now that he and Loring and Bert Millam were alone. 'Have you see Brownell in town tonight?'

Loring shook his head, remaining silent.

Jud said to Millam, 'Do you know Caleb Brownell the freighter?'

'Yes; at least I know who he is.'

'He was supposed to arrive here a half hour ago. Go see if you can find him.'

'You want him brought here?'

Jud nodded, turned away from young Millam as the youth started doorward for the second time this evening, and reached inside his coat for a cigar. He bit the tip off, struck a sulphur match, blew at the splutter of arcing light and billowing smoke, then lit up. Through this entire ritual Buck Loring continued to study Jud's face. Then he made a brusque headwag, emitted a little sigh and said, 'You're a hard man to figure out.'

'I'll be even harder when you hear what I want you to do, Buck.'

Jud proceeded then to tell Loring in a crisp, sharp voice, and for a full minute after he'd finished speaking Loring sat there like stone staring round-eyed upwards. He didn't move at all until the women re-entered the room. Then he started as though jabbed with a pin. At that selfsame moment the outer door swung open,

Bert Millam appeared in it, and trailing in his wake was Caleb Brownell.

'He was coming down the road,' said Millam, explaining the shortness of his absence to Jud. 'Had trouble with a horse or something and was delayed.'

Brownell moved uncomfortably deeper into the room. He viewed Mary Alice askance, his discomfort heightened considerably by her presence. Jud, noticing this and understanding its reason, bent to murmur something to his bride. Mary Alice immediately took Sharon with her and left the men alone with their coffee and their coffee cups.

Brownell nodded non-committally at Loring, hitched at his trousers and waited. Bert Millam was gazing at the pantry doorway oblivious to what occurred around him.

Jud said to Caleb Brownell: 'Did you make that payment?'

'I did. 'Matter of fact it was Miss Mary Alice who took the money and. . . .' Brownell paused to rummage in a shirt pocket. He held forth a slip of paper. '. . . Give me this receipt.'

Jud made no move to take the paper. Brownell put it slowly back into his pocket. The eyes of these two brawny men met and flintily held.

'As of now, Caleb, you aren't hauling any more freight into Seward City.'

Brownell's face did not alter expression

115

except up around the eyes. Here, there came to rest very ponderously, a craggy, dogged look, part defiance, part wonderment.

'Why not?'

'Because Seward City needs freight, that's why not.'

''Don't make sense,' growled the bearded freighter.

'In a week you'll find out how much sense it makes.'

'By then the whole town'll be hungry,' mumbled Brownell in the same tone, and raised a hand to the purple bruise high on his nose where Jud had smashed him senseless the second time they met.

'That's exactly the idea, Caleb.'

Brownell massaged his nose for a thoughtful moment then peered over at Jud doubtfully. 'I see what you're figurin' on doing all right. But Caldwell will *make* me haul freight.'

'How?'

Brownell shrugged. He shifted position and hitched at his trousers again. 'Caldwell knows ways,' he muttered. 'He'll get up some legal paper to seize my wagons. Then he'll commence hauling stuff in himself. Besides that, he'll hire men to. . . .'

'Not if he can't find your outfits, he won't.'

For a full sixty seconds no one in the room said a word. Then Brownell cast a suspicious glance at the pantry door. 'How about *her*; she's

116

his compadre.'

Now Buck Loring spoke. But first he slapped his leg and turned a look of dawning comprehension upon Jud Parker. 'Damn,' he cried out. '*That's* why you did it. Hey, Brownell—she's Jud Parker's wife.'

The bearded freighter's mouth fell open. He looked from Loring to Millam to Jud. 'Honest?' he squeaked. 'You mean Miss Mary Alice?'

Jud glowered at Loring. 'That's got nothing to do with it, you fool,' he growled. 'I could have worked this without. . . .'

'All right, all right,' soothed Loring, seeing Jud's wrathy look. 'But anyway she won't say anything to old Caldwell and that's the main thing.'

'She doesn't even work for Heber Caldwell any more,' rumbled Jud, not entirely mollified. 'She quit when the preacher closed his book.' He turned his sharpening attention back to the freighter. 'You get those damned freight outfits somewhere a long way off where Caldwell can't find them.'

'Where?' demanded Brownell. 'He'll have two dozen roughriders lookin' high an' low for me and them outfits as soon as the merchants begin wailing.'

'That's your part of this,' Jud retorted. 'And see you do a good job of it. Hide 'em and keep your crews out of Seward City.'

'For how long?'

117

'A week. Maybe two weeks. How the hell do I know how long it's going to take to get all these merchants who owe Caldwell money to start going broke? Maybe a month, Brownell.'

'Well, by golly,' exclaimed the freighter sharply. 'Who's going to pay their wages? I sure can't—not lyin' idle sixty, seventy miles back in the hills.'

Jud put aside his cigar, fished out a roll of bills, peeled off a dozen or so and pushed them into Brownell's hand. 'When that's used up come back for more. Not to town—to Loring's ranch.'

Buck immediately put in a sharp command. 'But doggone you, Brownell—don't you go setting up another camp on my range.'

Brownell ignored Loring, counted the money, pursed his lips into a silent whistle and looked up at Jud with clearing vision. He almost smiled. 'It'll be done like you say, Mister Parker. I'll have 'em emptied and movin' by dawn. Give me two days and I swear can't no Seward City hirelings of Heber Caldwell find me.' Caleb reverently stowed the money in his shapeless trousers. 'Anything else, Mister Parker?'

'Quit calling me "Mister Parker,"' growled Jud. 'Keep in touch with Loring at his ranch, but be careful about that. Caldwell might hire riders like you say. If he does you can bet they'll try to earn their money.'

'Sly like an Injun,' said Brownell. 'That's me.' He smiled for the first time since Jud had known him. It was a smile intended to make him look amiable but because of his shaggy great beard, sunk-set small eyes and battered face it succeeded only in making him look ferocious.

'Go on,' ordered Jud. 'Get your outfits rolling out.'

Brownell left the house.

Jud bent to put aside his cigar and Buck Loring said, 'What you asked me to do—you weren't serious were you? Jud; the law'll be boilin' out over the countryside like a bunch of Blackfeet bronco bucks.'

Jud measured Loring with a narrow glance. 'You want that mortgage back marked "paid in full" don't you?'

Loring arose; he paced once across the parlour and back again. He said in protest, 'Hell, Jud; if this thing backfires I'll be ruint. Caldwell'll wipe me out; maybe even get me lynched or something. And the law—there'll be deputy marshals swarmin' around like honey-bees.'

'Let 'em swarm. If you do the thing right they won't have anything to go on, Buck. Anyway, you aren't really doing anything terrible—just making out like you meant to.'

Loring stood there gazing steadily up into big Jud Parker's face. Moments later he returned to the chair, weakly sank down into it and

119

mumbled, 'I need a drink.'

'That's one thing you *don't* need. Keep your head clear, Buck.'

'Suppose we get caught?'

'I'll get you out of it.'

This seemed to cheer Loring a little. He shook his head wryly saying, 'All right. But you remember that: if anything backfires you're going to get me an' my boys clear.'

Jud made no reaffirmation of his earlier statement; he was already passing along to the next stage of his plan. 'Bert,' he barked, startling Millam from a tender reverie. 'Sharon goes home from here.'

Millam looked disbelieving. Gradually his expression became very pained. 'Jud; this is our wedding night. You can't do. . . .'

'*I said she goes home tonight!*'

Jud checked himself up short; he turned fully to face Millam. He spoke again, his voice softening towards the youth.

'Brownell needs at least ten hours to get well away, Bert. Buck here needs nearly as long to get his end of things set and ready. I don't want old Heber to suspect anything at least until tomorrow afternoon.' His tone softened still more, became both placating and parentally understanding. 'She can come to you at my hotel room at noon tomorrow. Then the two of you can get out of Seward City. I'll get a rig for you myself. I promise that, Bert.'

120

Millam nodded. 'All right,' he said. 'All right, Jud.' And he made a wan smile.

'Get her; see her safely home but don't let old Caldwell see you. Leave her to make it on to the house from the roadway. Then go to my hotel room and stay in there until I come along. Don't go out—not even to buy a drink at the Warbonnet to celebrate.'

Bert Millam arose. He nodded again in the same reluctant fashion. Jud flagged him away with an up-flung arm.

'Out of the back way with her.'

Only Jud and Buck Loring remained in Mary Alice's parlour. The transplanted Texan scooped his hat up from the floor, crushed it indifferently upon his head and also stood up. He was looking a little wonderingly at Jud Parker. 'If you pull this off someone'll write a book about you someday.'

'Goodnight,' growled Jud. 'I'll be in the Warbonnet tomorrow afternoon.'

'I'll be there,' said the rangeman and went forward to the door, stopped to cast a slow head-wag back at Jud, then passed out into the night.

Mary Alice swept into the smoke-layered parlour. She stopped to survey her man. He was standing motionless, completely oblivious of her nearness; completely engrossed with his thoughts.

Mary Alice went forward and brushed his arm with her fingers. Her cheeks were a deep scarlet.

'It's late, Jud.'

He turned. Gradually his brow cleared, his wilful eyes reached out to close down around her. He took a short forward step seeing her lovely, desirable. He bent slightly and found her mouth ready, warm and tender.

'Yes,' he said softly, 'it's late, Mary Alice.' He smiled his slow, infectious smile. Her eyes grew large and she also very slowly smiled.

'Whatever else being married to you will be like, Jud Parker, it will never be dull.'

He laughed at that.

Mary Alice turned away from him moving deeper into the house. He did not at once follow her. The night was still comparatively young. There were many things yet to consider, to plan ahead against. Then his rugged face broke into a full grin. Hell, he told himself, you can plan all night and the whole bluff will be decided by the flip of a coin anyway. He turned and went after her.

CHAPTER THIRTEEN

Mary Alice did not go to the bank. She instead remained home alone. Jud went to the hotel with the morning well along, found young Bert Millam pacing restlessly, and ordered breakfast sent up. He afterwards sat smoking at the

122

window hearing Millam eating behind him, and watching the flow of people passing in and out of old Heber Caldwell's bank. Occasionally he would lift his glance and fling it far out towards the undulating lift and fall of the far-away hills and mountains, as though by doing this he could pick up some faint sighting of Brownell's wagons.

He was carefully turning over in his mind something Mary Alice had told him several days earlier: That three of Seward City's prime storekeepers had notes due at the bank within the next ten days.

It had been this information which had brought him to the course he was now taking. He had not initially meant to move against Caldwell so rapidly; in fact, as he sat there now he was nagged at by small misgivings. He was a man who liked to carefully plan, meticulously prepare, be ready well in advance for all exigencies. He did not believe he'd done this now, and he was correct, he had not.

But the opportunity had been too good to let slip. Not only were the notes due, but in order to accumulate the money to meet them, these storekeepers had deliberately let their inventories get unprecedentedly low. Old Heber himself had learned this; had told Mary Alice of it with relish. She had said it appeared to please Heber greatly that this power over the merchants was so great, their fear of him so overpowering, that they feared being even one day late with their money.

Now Jud also felt pleased. Uneasy, perhaps, but also pleased. He had assessed Heber Caldwell with care and Jud Parker was a man who knew men. Old Caldwell cared for money and the power it gave him. He was avaricious beyond limit. As Jud had told Bert Millam, if you wished to destroy a man you had first to know his greatest weakness. Heber Caldwell's greatest weakness was greed.

Bert finished his belated breakfast, came across to where Jud sat looking down into Seward City's busy thoroughfare, and said, 'I don't think this day will ever end. Particularly the time between now and noon.'

Jud chuckled, removed his cigar and considered its flaky ash. 'She'll be along,' he said. 'She's a lovely girl. Beautiful. You know, when I first hit this town she knocked me down with her buggy. I thought then she was about the prettiest filly I'd ever seen.'

Bert, leaning upon the wall gazing down upon the sunlighted full width of Front Street, suddenly snapped erect. 'There she is,' he said breathlessly. 'At last she's coming.' He hastened to the door although Sharon had not as yet even turned into the hotel.

Jud watched her breasting the tide of rough men in her on-coming haste. He thought again that she was one of the most handsome women

124

he'd ever seen. He began to smile in a wintry way: Old Heber had lost his most precious jewel and didn't even know it!

Sharon turned into the hotel and Jud arose, put aside his cigar and absently smoothed his coat. He was looking doorward when Bert moved back and Heber Caldwell's daughter passed into the room. She was instantly swept into Millam's arms. They rocked together, Bert mumbling something against her hair and Sharon whimpering.

Jud crossed over to close the door.

'How is your father this morning, Mrs. Millam?'

She twisted in Bert's arms. Her eyes widened and darkened at sight of Jud. In a husky tone she said, 'I didn't see him. He was already retired when I got home last night and he was gone before I got up this morning.'

Jud passed back across to the window. It was nearly noon now; the roadway was emptying slightly and fewer people were entering the bank. Finally, conscious of stealthy sounds behind him he turned, saying, 'I'm going to get some cigars,' and left the room, went down to the hotel lobby and was crossing towards the street door when a well-dressed man halted athwart his path saying, 'Mister Parker?'

'Yes.'

'I'm Luce Shaeffer.'

Jud looked blank.

125

'I was with Miss Sharon the evening her rig knocked you down.'

'Oh yes,' said Jud, remembering this handsome face now. 'Sure; how are you?'

'I'm fine,' said Luce Shaeffer, in a tone that was silky. 'How are you?'

Jud heard something in these words that brought his guard up slowly. He said brusquely, 'What's on your mind, Shaeffer?'

'Possibly you didn't know, but I work for Mister Caldwell.'

Jud said nothing.

'He heard a rumour this morning at the bank. It seems one of the local preachers is supposed to have said he performed a double wedding ceremony last night.' Shaeffer's flawless face loosened into a rueful little grin. 'You supposedly married Miss Mary Alice Curry and a man named Millam allegedly married Mister Caldwell's daughter. Isn't that amusing, Mister Parker?'

'Very amusing,' growled Jud.

'Mister Caldwell sent me to find the man who is spreading the gossip with orders to stop it at once.'

'Have you found him?'

'No. He hitched up his wagon, loaded his family into it early this morning, and left town.'

Shaeffer's lingering smile lay now only down around his mouth. His eyes were steadily watching Jud's expression. He said, 'I can't for the life of me imagine why he was so frightened.'

'How do you know he was. Preachers have a way of going off somewhere to hold graveside services, baptisms, such like, Mister Shaeffer.'

'Taking all their household goods with them, Mister Parker?'

Jud shrugged. He glanced up at a wall clock. It was not quite one yet; this damned plump-handed and pale-faced bank clerk of Caldwell's could upset the applecart if he learned the truth too soon and carried it back to Heber. 'Come along,' he said to Shaeffer. 'I was just going to have a glass of ale. Between us we may be able to come up with an explanation of the preacher's behaviour.'

Shaeffer hesitated. He licked his lips and glanced at the people in the lobby. He did not want to be seen drinking with big Jud Parker, his employer's enemy.

'The minister's actions really don't concern me as much as. . . .'

'Come along,' said Jud, taking Shaeffer by the arm and leading him ahead. They passed along to the Warbonnet Saloon and each time someone looked up in astonishment at Jud Parker in company with Heber Caldwell's clerk, Luce Shaeffer winced.

At the bar, which was not as yet crowded, Jud flagged for service and turned to Shaeffer with a calculating look. 'Instead of looking for that

127

minister why didn't you go see Miss Sharon and Miss Mary Alice?'

'I did. That is, I went to Mister Caldwell's home to see Miss Sharon, but she wasn't there.'

'And Miss Mary Alice?' queried Jud, putting a coin into the barman's hand and sweeping up his tankard of ale. 'What did she say?'

'She wasn't home either. At least she didn't answer the door.'

Jud put his half-drained glass upon the bar, made a circuit of his lips with his tongue, then twisted towards Shaeffer. 'Kind of a mystery, isn't it?' he said blandly.

'Mister Caldwell doesn't like things like this.'

'I don't blame him.' Jud nodded towards the untouched glass in front of Luce Shaeffer. 'Drink up,' he said.

'I don't usually drink in the middle of the day.'

Jud smiled. 'This is a special occasion though.' Someone jostled him on the far side and he turned, throwing a casual glance in that direction.

'Hullo, Jud,' said Buck Loring. 'Hey bartender—an ale for me too.'

Jud turned back towards Shaeffer. 'Drink it down,' he repeated. 'I think I have the answer to your mystery for you.'

Luce Shaeffer dutifully drank. Jud continued to beam his steady smile upon the bank clerk. 'Good ale, isn't it?' he said. 'Sort of braces a man, doesn't it?'

Jud's bold stare was fixed upon Shaeffer. The clerk, sensing something between them, looked past where Buck Loring was lazily sipping, his head cocked in an attitude of listening. Beyond Loring were a number of other armed, rough-looking rangemen. They also were standing motionless with the elaborate casualness of men who were not in the least casual. Shaeffer licked his lips; he'd heard enough about big Jud Parker to become suddenly quite uneasy at his side.

'I suppose I'd better get back,' he murmured, and started to turn away.

'Before you know about the marriages?'

Shaeffer froze; Parker was inwardly laughing at him, he was sure of that. A terrible suspicion began to form in his brain. He hooked an elbow on the bar staring at Parker.

'Why don't you ask *me* about that rumour, Shaeffer?'

The clerk breathed a faint: 'No!'

Jud very slowly nodded. 'Yes,' he contradicted. 'It's the truth, Shaeffer. You remember Millam, don't you? Caldwell had him beaten and sent packing last year. Surely you remember that.'

'I remember.'

'He came back yesterday. Last night he married Caldwell's daughter. That preacher who lit out also married me to Miss Mary Alice.'

'Good Lord,' moaned the clerk. 'Mister

129

Caldwell. . . .'

'Yes? What'll Mister Caldwell do, Shaeffer?'

But the bank clerk did not hear. He drew away from the bar and began to slowly, almost drunkenly, make his way doorward.

At Jud's side Buck Loring said, 'Did you remember to get Millam out of town?'

'No,' Jud replied crisply. 'Come on; we'll do that right now.'

Loring caught Jud's arm and held him there. 'It's too late now. He wouldn't get two miles off before Caldwell'd have roughriders track him down and kill him.'

'Like hell,' snarled Jud. 'Come on.'

He and Buck Loring hastened up to the hotel room. They were met in the doorway by Bert himself. After he'd heard Jud out he shook his head saying, 'I never had any intention of leaving Seward City like that, Jud. That was your idea, not mine.'

Buck closed the hotel room door, and leaned upon it. Across the room sitting at the window was Sharon. She was listening to her husband argue with big Jud Parker and was mortally afraid for him because Parker's face was angryred.

'You damned fool, he'll explode when he hears you 'n his girl are married.'

'Then let him explode. He can't undo the marriage.'

'Fat lot of good that'll do Miss Sharon if

130

you're dead,' growled Jud. Then threw up his hands, saying, 'All right; stay. We can't spend the rest of this day arguing. We've got work to do.'

From the door Loring said: 'What about Miss Mary Alice? 'You reckon he might be mad enough to try something against her?'

Jud faced Loring, his face like iron. 'I don't think he's that foolish, Buck. Anything like that would be fatal for him.'

Buck nodded, looking swiftly away from the leashed violence in the big man's eyes. 'I reckon he'd know that,' he murmured. Then straightened up off the door.' 'My boys are ready, Jud, as soon as the sun sets.'

CHAPTER FOURTEEN

In Seward City violence was no novelty, but organised violence in the fashion Heber Caldwell planned it, was unprecedented.

He had, as Jud had predicted, literally exploded when Luce Shaeffer had returned to the bank and told him what he'd learned from Jud Parker himself. At first, though, old Caldwell had doubted; had felt that Parker was deliberately baiting him. Then, after a stormy visit to Mary Alice's house when, in a moment of blinding fury he'd raised his hand against

131

Mary Alice in near-violence, old Heber had raced back to his bank.

'I want that man killed!' he roared at Shaeffer. 'I want you to go hire me five of the toughest men you can find in the saloons. Bring them back here with you. I want that damned scoundrel dead at my feet.'

Luce Shaeffer, quivering in the face of such wrath, had asked tremulously, 'Which man, Mister Caldwell; Parker or Millam?'

'*Parker*, you simpleton! *Jud Parker*. He's behind this; he made Sharon do that. He's a devil. I'll pay a thousand dollars for him dead at my feet and I don't care how it's done. Now get out of here—go get me those toughs and be quick about it!'

Luce Shaeffer had had no difficulty finding five men willing to kill for a thousand dollars, but Shaeffer had made an understandable error; he had originally sought them in the Warbonnet Saloon, and afterwards he'd been quietly trailed from one drinking house to another by Loring's riders, and when he'd ultimately recruited them Loring's men knew who the toughs were and carried this news to Buck at the hotel.

To this information Jud said: 'Fine,' and went to the window to gaze across at the bank, then, calculatingly, at the lowering, reddening late sun. To Bert Millam and Sharon he said, 'One of Loring's men will take you out to his ranch. You'll stay there.'

132

Millam protested. Jud heard him out with a searching look at Sharon, then gruffly ordered Millam to stay with Caldwell's daughter. 'You likely won't miss anything,' he stated. 'They'll be looking for you hard and might just find you too. If it's excitement you want, boy, you just might get it out there.'

To Buck he said: 'This trouble will occupy Heber the rest of the day. You go back to the saloon with your boys and stay there. So far he probably hasn't linked you with me. You know what to do after sunset.'

Loring departed. Jud watched him go with mixed emotions, then he sighed, returned to the window and said no more until a small body of rough men emerged from the bank, paused a moment to briefly converse at roadside, and afterwards split up to go their separate ways through town.

Jud faced away from the window. To Bert Millam he said, 'We're going to have a caller or two pretty quick now. The hirelings are beginning their search for me.'

Millam looked uncertainly at Sharon. She was very pale and very large-eyed. 'Come,' he said, taking her hand. 'There's another room to this suite.'

When he'd left her, Millam returned to Jud's side, casually unbuttoned his coat and cast a slow, hard glance at the larger man. 'Wish it was old Heber himself coming up here,' he said

133

quietly.

'No. You don't want anything like that. He's her father. Remember that. Besides, this is more my fight than yours.'

'Pretty big odds though,' murmured the younger man.

Jud smiled. 'It's not going to be easy as they think. Buck has orders too.'

Jud did not clarify this nor did Bert Millam ask him to for that moment a rough set of knuckles struck the outer door.

Millam moved back away from the door to the centre of the room. His face was tough-set and his eyes were drawn-out-narrow. Jud moved forward easily, threw back the door and gazed flintily at the two rough men standing there. 'Come in,' he growled at them. 'I've been expecting you.'

They moved into the room, one stopping almost at once as he spied Bert Millam and Millam's spread-legged stance. A sharp warning passed this man's lips to his companion and the second man also halted to throw a swift look ahead at Millam. Both these men were armed and capable looking.

'How much am I worth to your boss?' queried big Jud Parker.

The shorter of the two toughs said nothing; he was warily concentrating upon Bert Millam. The larger man said curtly, 'A thousand dollars dead.'

134

'You won't collect it,' growled Jud, then proceeded to carefully remove his coat, fold it and lay it gently upon the bed. 'In fact you won't be healthy enough to even try and collect it.' He levelled a finger at the largest man. 'You first. Take off that gun!'

The big man's glance darted past to Millam. It went fully around the room and came again to settle upon Jud Parker. 'No,' this man muttered, his face reddening. 'I ain't goin' to fight you, Parker. I seen what you did to Caleb Brownell.'

'You're not going to have that choice,' retorted Jud, moving closer. 'Caldwell's men made a bargain and I'm here to see they keep it.'

'No,' reiterated the large man a second time, moving back, giving way before Jud's approach. 'I'll gun-fight you, Parker, but not fist-fight you.'

The shorter of Caldwell's two hirelings spoke now for the first time. He was no longer gazing ahead where Bert Millam stood; he was looking over his shoulder at the silent men who suddenly appeared in the opened doorway. Rangemen, these were, and one of them was methodically chewing a cud of tobacco, his thumbs hooked in a shell-belt, his unwavering, hard eyes fixed forward in an impassively flinty face.

'Forget it,' this man said in an unnaturally rising voice. 'Forget it, Mister Parker. We know

135

when we got hold o' the short end o' the stick. To hell with Caldwell; never had much use for him nohow.'

His companion also sighted the watching men in the doorway. On an out-rushing breath he concurred, saying rapidly, 'I quit. Just now I quit workin' for Caldwell. We didn't figure on nothin' like this a-tall.'

'What did you figure on?' demanded Jud.

'Well; Caldwell said it'd be only you and maybe this young feller here.'

Jud nodded. Caldwell as yet knew nothing of Loring's or Brownell's part in his feud with big Jud Parker and that was the way Jud had planned it. He made a wintry smile. He went over and plucked away the guns these two men wore and gestured towards chairs with them. 'Sit down. Tie them, Bert.' To the men at the door he said, 'Where's Buck?'

'Downstairs waitin',' answered the tobacco-chewing rider in a quiet drawl, moving his eyes just enough to also include Jud in their line of vision.

'Tell him to find the other three and bring them up here.'

The rangeman departed, pacing casually downstairs out of sight. One of his friends who remained at the door moved up to fill in the vacancy this man's departure had created, and began leisurely to twist up a cigarette.

Within ten minutes Buck Loring and his rider

came clumping up to Jud's room herding along Caldwell's remaining three hirelings. At the door, watching Bert Millam go over these additional prisoners for weapons, Loring said, 'Caldwell's got the Marshal searching for his girl too. I heard him say old Caldwell swore out a warrant against you, Jud.'

Parker crossed over to the window and gazed down into the roadway. An inexperienced observer might not have noticed the little cliques of conversing people gathered here and there speaking excitedly among themselves; Jud noticed them. He considered particularly the group in front of the bank and he smiled to himself. There was one thing you could say about Seward City—news travelled by word of mouth faster than a telegraph could have carried it. He faced back into the room. Early evening's spreading shadows lay thickeningly behind him over rooftops and farther out, where the flowing endlessness of land ran on to a meeting with the mountains. In a voice strongly deep he said to Buck Loring, 'It's about time. We'll leave Caldwell's lads here. Better get going, Buck.'

Loring, peering past, out the window, nodded soberly. 'Yeah, he muttered, and turned. 'Come on, boys.'

Jud lit a cigar. When it was going well he said to Bert Millam, 'You'd better leave now too. It's dark enough. Go out the back way, get a rig and don't waste any time.' He dropped his gaze to

137

the impasively watching faces of his prisoners, considered each man in his turn, and made a faint frown. 'The worst mistakes men like you make—and men like old Caldwell—is underestimating other men. You thought all you had to do, to earn that lousy thousand dollars, was walk up behind me somewhere and shoot.'

Only one of the toughs had anything to say. This man puckered up his eyes and self-consciously grinned. 'I never had that notion,' he said. 'I had in mind givin' you a chance.'

'What kind of chance?'

The tough's smile turned raffish. 'A chance to pay me five hundred *not* to shoot you.'

'You were losing money,' Jud growled contemptuously.

'Naw I wasn't. Caldwell's finished. Maybe he don't know it an' maybe most other folks hereabouts don't know it. But I know it.'

Jud's attention centred upon this man. His scowl deepened. He had the feeling that somewhere he'd seen this man before. 'Go on,' he ordered this man. 'What's the rest of it?'

'You'd be a good man to work for, after you've taken over this town. You were a good man to work for layin' rail back in Missouri, Mister Parker. I worked for you on the track-layin' gang of the Western Pacific Railroad. 'Course, that's been six years back—but a feller doesn't easy forget a man like you.' This unkempt, raffish man smiled boldly up into

138

Jud's face. 'Caldwell don't know you—yet. I do; you'll beat him and I'd be a heap better off takin' your five hundred dollars than takin' his one thousand. I'd still be around when Caldwell wasn't and so would you; I'd work for you again. You see?'

Jud smoked in thoughtful silence. It was odd how a man on the way up encountered other men who were anxious to tie their own ambitions to the tail of the rising man's star, even in a place like the Dakotas. Looking into that raffish, lean and unshaven face he knew this other man was down on his luck. He also recognised feral craftiness when he saw it. He could depend upon men such as this only as long as he was on top. If he lost a little prestige, a little power or strength, these were the same 'friends' who would connive secretly with his enemies to expedite his downfall.

Jud found nothing disillusioning in this at all, for he was also an opportunist who had no time for failure, so after a time he removed the cigar and bent a hard, slow smile upon this man.

'You can start working for me now,' he said. 'But not for five hundred dollars—for two hundred.'

The raffish man wiggled his shoulders. 'Untie me. You got yourself a good man.'

Jud cut the bonds and watched as the former Caldwell hireling massaged his wrists. 'Their guns are on the bed,' he told the released man.

'Keep them here.'

'Sure, Mister Parker, but for how long?'

Jud looked at his watch then turned to stare downward where darkness was swiftly falling. 'Until all hell busts loose,' he said, snapping the watch closed, returning it to his pocket.

The raffish man seemed to understand, for he said next, 'And after that—what do I do?'

'Just stay out of the way and keep your eyes open. Seward City's going to be an unhealthy place by midnight.'

Jud caught up his coat, donned it and went to the door. Another of Caldwell's men stopped him there with a question.

'Mister Parker; 'you need another man?'

Jud shook his head, saying, 'No; but I'll give you lads a little advice. I never forget a face or an enemy. When you fellows get loose the smartest thing you can do is get on the stage and head for Leadville, or maybe even some place even farther than that. Like Miles City, Montana, for instance, or Independence.'

He looked back where the raffish man was leaning upon the wall, a pistol dangling from the fingers at his side, ironically smiling at his former companions.

'When this is all over hunt me up and I'll pay you.'

'I'll do that, Mister Parker. You can bank on it, I'll do that.'

Jud softly closed the door, moved along to the

head of the stairway, and paused there to cast a keen, rummaging look down into the lobby. A few men were sitting there, lounging, but there was not a single face he recognised so he began the descent. Afterwards, alive to Loring's warning about the Town Marshal's having a warrant for him, he passed out of the hotel through the kitchen and went stealthily down a refuse-laden dark alleyway as far as a parting between two dark and silent buildings. There, he went forward to a juncture with Front Street, and leaned in dense darkness smoking and expectantly watching Heber Caldwell's now dark and steel-barred bank.

It was, by Jud's gold watch, nine minutes to nine o'clock.

CHAPTER FIFTEEN

At exactly nine o'clock a terrific explosion rocked Seward City. Into the echoing tumult of this great blast came the startled cries of men, the terrified screams of horses, and a regular bedlam of barking dogs, running feet, and loud shouts.

From where Jud was standing it was as though something with incredible brightness had lit up the entire city from over behind Caldwell's bank.

141

Moments later came the oily smoke and acrid stench. Jud watched a solitary cloud of dark dust rise up and hang in the night air. He heard flying gravel rain down upon roofs and saw men ducking to escape this pelting deluge.

He smiled, chewed his cigar, and after a time moved smoothly across to the liverybarn, entered it, found no one around, harnessed a horse into the shafts of a top-buggy and drove quietly out into the roadway, cut northward as far as the edge of town, then lashed the animal into a trot and navigated the byways until he at last arrived before Mary Alice's house. Here, he did not have to enter for Mary Alice was standing outside with a shaken look upon her face, and at sight of Jud alighting she ran down to him, throwing herself into his arms. He put her bodily into the buggy, got in beside her and drove away, making again that identical wide circle which brought him again to the northernmost limit of Seward City. There he drew down and handed her the lines.

'Go out to Loring's place,' he told her. 'Wait for me there.'

'Jud; come with me! Please. . . .'

'I'll be along.'

'What *was* that explosion?'

'A little dynamite,' he said, caressing her hands. 'Go on now, Mary Alice.'

'Did you?. . . ?'

'No, I didn't set it off. But I knew it was

142

going to be set off. Now go on, Mary Alice.'

'Jud! You can't stay in Seward City. Mister Caldwell was by the house. He said all sorts of things about you. He's going to. . . .'

'Never mind all that now,' interrupted Jud, hearing the roar of voices back in town. 'You just do like I say and I'll be along when I can get away.'

He stepped back, struck the animal upon the rump and made a little salute as Mary Alice was borne northward, lines lying loose in her hands. Somewhere, well west of where he was standing, was the unmistakable sound of a number of speeding horsemen also heading north. He listened a moment, then made a satisfied nod of his head and started slowly back down towards the centre of town, keeping always well in the shadows and strong, shielding darkness.

From the shelter of a narrow building-well between two stores he watched the milling, shouting press of men surging forward around the bank. There was a lingering scent of cordite in the air as well as the stronger taste of dust. If Buck Loring had set the charge as Jud had instructed him to, the rear wall of Caldwell's bank should be just about demolished.

Six men charged up wearing five-pointed stars upon their shirts. Each of these men was armed with a sawed-off shotgun. One of these men detailed the others so that a cordon was speedily established completely around the

143

bank. Then this same man went up under the overhang of Caldwell's building and cried out loudly to the crowd.

'Leave off,' the Town Marshal bellowed. 'Go on home, boys. We got everything in hand now.'

'The hell you have,' roared a bearded miner. 'What about our gold—our money?'

'We'll find out when Mister Caldwell gets here. Now go on home, boys. Don't loiter around here.'

Some of the crowd dispersed but a great number of men moved only as far away as the opposite side of the roadway, and there came together in gatherings of various size to angrily gesticulate and speak out. Jud heard them easily; mostly, these men were miners and merchants. They were convinced there had been an actual bank robbery and were wailing over anticipated losses. Several times Jud heard Heber Caldwell's name mentioned grimly; he even heard one man exclaim angrily that he thought Caldwell might even have engineered the robbery himself.

Caldwell arrived himself, hastily dressed and grey-faced, no more than twenty minutes after the Marshal had taken charge at the scene. Jud saw Heber seek out the Marshal at once, speak swiftly to him, then be led round the back by the lawman. Neither the Marshal or old Heber reappeared.

Jud crossed eventually to the liverybarn, hired a horse from a round-eyed night-hostler, and leisurely left Seward City by the north roadway. He knew the hostler would waste no time seeking the Marshal with this information so he rode slowly, conserving the horse, until sometime later he heard riders pounding along in his wake. Then he swung westward and halted long enough to strike a sulphur match to a cigar, make sure the possemen had seen this and had veered in hot pursuit, then he lifted the livery animal into a long lope, reversed his course, and rode the full long distance to Loring's Pothook Ranch with only infrequent pauses to blow the horse. He had effectively lost the posse; he had also smoked his last cigar.

Loring's functionally ugly home was ablaze with lights as Jud came into sight of it. He was crossing onward towards this constant lodestar when a horseman came out of darkness on either side of him saying nothing and accompanied him the remaining distance forward. When he dismounted one of these men turned, spat an amber stream aside, and nodded gravely.

'They're waitin' inside, Mister Parker.' The rangeman shifted his cud, smiled, and added: 'That was the dangdest explosion ever I seen. Liked to scairt my horse plumb out o' the country.'

Jud went onward to enter the house. Inside, he at once noticed a fifth member among those

145

including Mary Alice, Buck Loring, Bert and Sharon, who gazed steadily and silently upon him. It was Caleb Brownell. He frowned at him saying, 'What are you doing here?'

Brownell shrugged self-consciously. 'I was waitin' around when these folks come a-riding. No harm in that, is there?'

'Where are the wagons and crews?'

'Where can't no busybody find 'em unless I take him there.'

'You're supposed to be there too, in case your crews get restless and decide to ride into town.'

'Not likely,' said Brownell succinctly. 'I put two men to seein' that don't happen.'

'Get back out there with them anyway,' snapped Jud.

'Wait a minute,' Loring put in at this juncture. 'It might be a good idea for him to hang around, Jud. With you'n Millam, me an' my three riders we've got only six men here—in case of real trouble.'

'What trouble? Seward City's got no leadership right now and as near as I can figure out, no one to rightfully blame for the way you blew the back out of the bank.'

'Yeah, but that isn't going to stay that way for long. Caldwell'll know you're behind that someway.'

'He probably will,' agreed Jud. 'And let him.' He jerked his head at Caleb Brownell. 'Get out of here; go back to your camp and stay there at least until tomorrow night.'

Brownell left.

Jud said to Loring, 'I'm hungry,' and edged past towards Loring's unkempt kitchen. There, he halted to make a grimace. 'I guess I'm not hungry after all,' he grumbled.

Bert Millam laughed. They all turned their eyes towards him. Mary Alice, understanding too, smiled and arose. 'Sharon....' The two women went to work in the kitchen and Jud passed back across the outer room to a chair.

'What was it like?' asked Buck Loring. Then said with a great wag of his head, 'I'll tell you one thing—five sticks was too cussed much. It liked to blew us clean out of our saddles and we were near the edge of town when it went off.'

Jud told them, speaking graphically, and afterwards not a one of them said a word until the women came back with hot coffee and food. Then Bert Millam fixed a lively look upon Jud asking what they would do next.

Jud ate and talked and drank coffee. He had not known the exact extent of his hunger until Mary Alice had set food before him; he found himself thoroughly famished.

'Move fast,' he said to them. 'For one thing those men we left at the hotel will be free by now. Caldwell will know Loring is in this with us and he'll have the law out here by dawn.'

Buck's mouth fell open. 'You didn't turn them loose did you?'

147

'Did you expect me to shoot them?'

Loring continued to stare at Jud. 'Caldwell will. . . .'

'No he won't,' Jud cut in swiftly. 'We have the initiative and we're going to keep it. By sunup you're going to send in whichever of your riders weren't at the hotel and weren't seen by those hirelings of Caldwell's.'

'What for?'

'They're going to go from saloon to saloon spreading the rumour that there's to be another attempt to rob the bank.'

Jud's audience looked blankly at him. He did not finish speaking until he'd drained off the last of his coffee.

'They'll believe it. Obviously someone attempted to rob the bank tonight and didn't have time to follow through with it after dynamiting the building. When the rumour gets around there'll be a run on Caldwell; I think darned few folks with money in his bank won't be clamouring for a withdrawal.'

'Break him?' queried Bert Millam.

Jud shook his head. 'A man like Caldwell can't be broken that easily, but he sure can be pushed to the edge of panic.'

Beyond the parlour Jud could hear Sharon and Mary Alice murmuring together. He could not distinguish their words and knew that neither could they distinguish what he was saying. He did not, really, have any qualms

148

about Sharon, yet he wanted to spare her as much of this plotting against her father as he could.

'All right,' said Loring, cutting across Jud's thoughts. 'I can send two men to town no one will suspect was with us last night. But that rumour might not cause a lot of damage.'

'It doesn't have to cause damage,' explained Jud. 'All it has to do is keep old Caldwell reeling.'

'Reeling: How—reeling?'

'Yesterday morning he lost Mary Alice, his right arm. Yesterday noon he lost his daughter and at the same time learnt a man he had beaten a year ago was back in town wearing a gun. Yesterday afternoon he discovered his worst enemy had married his secretary; he would guess from that no secret his secretary knew about him was any longer a secret. And last night—or tonight if you prefer—his bank was dynamited.'

Loring and Bert Millam were both nodding. Millam said: 'Now the rumour, the run on his bank, and—what else?'

'A couple more little surprises,' mumbled Jud, getting heavily upright. 'Right now we need a little sleep.' He gazed upon Buck. 'Married folks ought to have the house, don't you agree?'

The rangeman got up out of his chair with a lopsided grin. 'That's usually the custom,' he said, moving doorward. 'But I'll roust you out before sunup.'

'With fresh horses,' said Jud.

Loring nodded and passed out into the late night.

CHAPTER SIXTEEN

Before dawn they swept out of Loring's yard in a party, Loring's three riders scouting on ahead at Jud's orders. By the time they were within sight of Seward City a faint pink light lay over everything and Jud now sent the pair of rangemen forward into town whom no one there could associate with the trouble of the night before.

He then beckoned Buck and the remaining Pothook horsemen up close and instructed them to ride to as many outlying ranches as they could reach this day, and say that the food supplies in town were running low and that because Caldwell had bankrupted Caleb Brownell it was unlikely additional supplies would arrive in Seward City for perhaps thirty days.

Finally, he told Bert Millam to take his wife and Mary Alice back to Mary Alice's home and remain with them there. To this Sharon made an impassioned protest saying her father would find them and send men to kill her husband.

'Your father won't have time for that,' replied Jud impatiently, and looked over Sharon's head at Bert, making a gesture. Millam came forward to remove Sharon. Mary Alice also came forward. She stopped beside Jud without speaking, saw the flash of his stare, and reached over gently to lay a hand briefly upon his arm.

'Be careful, Jud,' was all she said.

He left them, riding slowly onward towards Seward City, then he swung easterly and rode far out with one eye upon the lifting sun of this new day. He halted, wishing he had a cigar to aid in killing the necessary time, then forgot the cigar entirely when he spied a host of mounted men swirl rapidly northward out of town beating up a plume of fine dust. This, he correctly deduced, was a posse bound for the Pothook.

He waited fully two hours before approaching town from off in the east; heard the angry hum of many voices, too, long before he came into shadows behind town and got down from the livery animal. From a vantage point between two buildings he saw the near-riot boiling along Front Street, and moments later when this jostling great horde of people hit Caldwell's bank, the emergence from this crowd of a harassed Town Marshal and his little clutch of deputies, once more struggling for order and carrying riot-guns.

He passed around behind this shouting mass

and moved into the deserted Warbonnet Saloon. There, a startled bartender looked upon him with widening eyes.

'Cigars,' ordered Jud, lit one, exhaled, held the barman's gaze with his own steady regard, and said, 'And an ale.'

The drink came and with it some swiftly spoken advice. 'Mister Parker; the Marshal's been hunting high an' low for you. He's got a warrant.'

'So I heard,' murmured Jud, draining off the ale and putting aside the glass. 'What's the trouble over at the bank?'

'Folks want their money out of it.'

'That's their right.'

The barman's anxiety lessened in the face of Jud's massive calm. He scratched the tip of his nose, then sighed. 'I guess it is. Maybe a feller can't blame 'em either. Folks hereabouts work pretty hard for their money. There's strong talk goin' around those bandits who tried to dynamite their way in last night and got scairt off will will try again.'

'They might at that.'

The barman nodded. 'Mister Parker; old Caldwell's out for your topknot. There's a rumour he's posted a thousand dollars for you dead.'

'He's going to be too busy to worry about me,' said Jud.

The barman craned his neck and peered past

Jud into the yonder roadway. 'Word sure spreads fast,' he opined. 'Look-a-there miners and rangemen comin' in with wagons.'

Jud looked, smoked slowly, and was only a little surprised that Buck Loring had been so successful with the outlying settlers; Buck *did* have a persuasive personality.

Now Front Street was choked with agitated people, for no sooner had the people coming for supplies been told of the run on Caldwell's bank, than they also joined it. Over the tumult rose the Marshal's strong voice turned knife-edged with harassment. Jud paid and left the Warbonnet, went unobtrusively around behind the eastern side of Front Street and slow-paced along the alleyway there as far as the largest mercantile store in Seward City. There, entering by a rear door unobserved, he stood in dim shadows watching clerks and customers clamouring at each other. At this rate, he thought, Seward City would be devoid of saleable merchandise before nightfall. He passed back out into the alleyway again and stood there smoking. Stood there listening to disconnected sentences being shouted back and forth in a din of excitement which had in his experience no equal.

There were a number of fights, spontaneous affairs which were speedily localised by the perspiring special deputies. There was at least one run-away, and this cleared the roadway with greater alacrity than the Marshal and all his recruits ever could have done; the team raced south the full length of Front Street and passed beyond town in a jerking spiral of dust. Behind them rode two hastily mounted and profanely shouting horsemen, whip-arms rising and falling.

Jud stepped into sunlight to cast an appraising glance skyward. It was a little past high noon. He strolled along to the rear of the hotel and entered. There wasn't a soul in the kitchen, the pantry, or the dining-room. There was only one man in the lobby and he was holding to the doorjamb quivering with excitement and staring with a breathless expression out into the roadway. Jud passed over behind him and steadily mounted to his room. There, surrounded by the hush of an empty building, he drew over a chair near the window and sat down to watch the turmoil down below from this most excellent vantage point.

Far beyond Seward City dust-devils jerked to life by the feet of on-coming horses gave an impression of a prairie fire. Horsemen and wagoners were converging from several directions. The only quietude which Jud saw in all this uproar was in the avenues beyond, where deserted roadways and quiet residences lay. He sought for and found without much trouble the house where Mary Alice was waiting with

Sharon and Bert Millam. This was the quietest sector and for that he was grateful.

Down below a man in an eye-catching white apron and ornate sleeve-garters was fighting his way towards the Town Marshal. Jud recognised this man at once; his eyes followed this man with cold interest; saw him reach the Marshal in front of the bank, and cry out loudly in an almost vain effort to capture the lawman's attention.

It was the barman from the Warbonnet.

Jud had no doubt at all about what the barman was yelling to the Marshal. He saw the lawman finally twist, look into the barman's face, then bend a little the better to hear what was being yelled at him, and afterwards straighten up with a ramrod stiffness. Words passed his lips and the barman began to gesticulate. The Marshal went quickly to another man wearing a badge, spoke into his ear curtly, then stepped down into the roadway and began to roughly, almost savagely, shoulder his way through the crowd. At his heels the bartender followed closely enough to escape most of the jostling.

Jud removed his cigar, cast a final flinty gaze at Heber Caldwell's swamped bank, and arose to cross over and halt near the door. He missed seeing several other men in white aprons begin to filter forward through the crowd because he did this; these were merchants who had heard, at long last, of the impending shortage of supplies and how this had come to pass, and were now irately struggling towards the bank to demand of Heber Caldwell if he had, as rumour had it, deliberately bankrupted Caleb Brownell, because if he had, they knew, he had thereby also bankrupted them. Such was their knowledge and regard of Caldwell that they were beginning to think he had deliberately done this to them also, in order to force them out of business. He already owned most of their buildings; they thought now that it was additionally his plan to own their businesses as well.

Jud knew nothing of this; at least he did not know that this part of his scheme was also progressing according to his hopes, because, as these merchants were fighting for entrance to the bank, Seward City's fiercely moustached Town Marshal hit the door of his room with a powerful shoulder and burst into the room gun in hand.

Jud let the lawman catch his balance before he spoke from behind him, and then he addressed not the Marshal but the curious barman who was following the lawman into his room.

'Get out of here,' Jud said very evenly to the barman, and called him two unprintable names. The bartender stumbled backwards and Jud closed the door upon him, turning as he did towards the Marshal.

156

'Parker; you are under arrest!'

'All right,' said the larger of these two men. 'For what?'

'Are you armed, Parker?'

'No. What am I arrested for?'

'Coercing a young girl.'

'Sharon Caldwell?'

'That's right!'

'Marshal; Miss Sharon is of the age of legal consent. Anyway, *I* didn't marry her, Bert Millam did. And they were married right and proper by an authorised clergyman.'

'She didn't have her paw's consent to get married.'

'She didn't need it.'

Jud returned the Marshal's steadily hostile gaze with a look equally as steady but with no rancour showing in it at all.

'Anything else, Marshal?'

With a stilted motion the lawman returned his weapon to its holster. He gestured towards the street below where the shouting and scuffling appeared to have reached a crescendo.

'You're responsible for that, too. Mister Caldwell told me so.'

'Mister Caldwell,' said Jud, without raising his voice, 'hates my guts. Before this is through he'll probably try and say I robbed his bank.'

'It wasn't robbed!' said the Marshal with some heat. 'How many times do I have to say that, anyway! Not a dime was taken. The bandits were scairt off.'

Jud moved easily across in front of the Marshal and halted where he could gaze down into the road. 'I guess you haven't been very convincing,' he murmured. 'Look down there.'

'Look hell,' swore the perspiring lawman. 'I just came from down there.'

Jud swung around. His eyes were narrowed to pinpoints and fire lay banked in their deepest depths. 'Marshal; let's you and me go talk to old Caldwell. I've got a few things to discuss with him and I'd like to have you hear them—and also hear his answers.' Jud changed suddenly, loosening in his stance, in his stony regard, even in his address. 'Caldwell is a man whose word is worth nothing unless it's on paper or spoken before witnesses. I want you for that witness.'

The Marshal drew back a big breath and slowly expelled it. He bent a long and searching look upon Jud. Then he began to bewilderedly wag his head back and forth.

'All I want is for this damned town to calm down. If you an' old Caldwell can accomplish that I'll be a witness for both of you. But I'll tell you one thing, Mister Parker: If Heber Caldwell stepped out into that roadway right now they'd tear him to pieces and if I had a dozen more special deputies I couldn't save him.'

Jud gave the Marshal his slow, hard smile. He said, 'You know something, Marshal? If I was standing with you at his side I wouldn't lift a

158

hand to keep him from being torn to pieces. Now let's go.'

They passed together from the room, descended into the lobby and were at once surrounded by a crowd of men whose agitated faces, damp with sweat, emphasised their unintelligible clamourings.

The Marshal held up a hand. 'Hold it,' he cried. 'Shut up! One at a time.'

This having no effect, Jud reached forward swiftly, caught two of the men, lifted them off the ground one in each mighty fist, and shook them like rag dolls. This astonishing evidence of Jud's great strength struck onlookers silent; they stepped clear and Jud tossed away his captives.

'Now one of you say your piece,' he growled at them. 'Just one.

A fiery-headed miner took one step forward saying loudly, 'He's going to close the back for today. Old Caldwell's going to close up until tomorrow. He sent Shaeffer out to tell us that. 'Said he'd open again in the mornin' but didn't want us all crowdin' in after sundown—what with the bank busted into and all.'

The Marshal looked at Jud. 'Go on,' he said to him. 'I'll have to stand guard at the door. Even then I don't like it, Parker. These people might riot.'

'Tell them,' answered Jud from a stiffening mouth, 'that old Caldwell *won't* close that bank

159

until every one of them that wants his lousy money out gets it out. Tell them Jud Parker guarantees that.'

He shoved roughly through and strode powerfully out into the lowering shadows of late afternoon. Where he had to, in order to make headway, he brought up his fists and battered a path onward.

Dead ahead near the fringe of the howling, fist-waving mob, loomed an armed deputy marshal. Jud set his course for this man and thrust ahead without hesitation. Around him men flung around cursing at Jud's merciless pummelling. They broke off their profanity at sight of his craggy face, at the sight of his raised, big scarred fists, then fell away before him. A few but not many knew him by sight and called out as he passed.

'That's Jud Parker. That's the feller old Caldwell's tryin' to get killed.'

'Parker? Hey, Parker? You goin' in there to bust his stinkin' skull?'

'Go on, Parker; give it to the old devil. Give it to him good!'

A rugged face barred Jud's way. It was the deputy and he had his riot-gun lowered, half pointing at Jud. He started to speak. Jud wrenched the gun away and spun the man around as he passed him. Then he snarled: 'Let 'em continue to come in a few at a time; old Caldwell isn't closing *this* bank!' He threw the

160

deputy's gun back at him, waved to the crowd and passed on inside.

A mighty shout of approval went up in his rear.

CHAPTER SEVENTEEN

Inside Heber Caldwell's bank there were armed guards standing impassively around the room. Several of these men were also armed with shotguns but most had only sidearms. It was their presence which kept the people standing in ranks before the counter orderly and more or less quiet.

Behind the counter were the clerks, Luce Shaeffer among them, who were working rapidly at accommodating these sweaty customers. Jud saw Shaeffer's head lift, his eyes dart over the crowd, find Jud and widen enormously at sight of him. Jud moved past towards Heber Caldwell's private office. From his edge of vision he saw Shaeffer move swiftly to intercept him. Shaeffer called quickly to one of the armed men. Jud kept on, reached Caldwell's office door and pushed on with scarcely any break in his long stride.

In Caldwell's office there were two men, old Heber at the desk and a bullish man with a shotgun who was standing back discreetly behind and slightly off to one side of Caldwell. At Jud's abrupt entrance both men jumped their glances to the doorway. Jud saw Heber half rise from his chair and hang there; eyes as cold as ice, as pale and as lifeless, fix themselves upon him.

Behind Caldwell the bodyguard started to lift his riot-gun. 'Leave it be,' growled Jud to this latter man. The shotgun grew still in the guard's two hands. 'Stay out of this,' commanded Jud, then transferred his hard look to the banker. 'Sit back down,' he ordered, and Caldwell sank down again. His face was grey, the lips thin and bloodless. He stared at big Jud Parker as he might have at an angry bear. In the face of Jud's challenging expression he stiffened unnaturally in the chair, strongly silent.

Caldwell had belief in himself; a kind of confidence fifty years of financial triumph had instilled in him. Now all this began to crumble. It had been cracking now for twenty-four hours and Jud's presence hastened the disintegration. Jud saw this subtle changing; witnessed Caldwell's inner fright begin to show in those very pale eyes, the old miser's spirit unequal to the issue confronting him. He went ahead to lean upon old Heber's desk; to watch old Caldwell's manhood dissolve. Sharp lines of distaste formed around Jud's mouth. Caldwell, facing his own ruin, his admiration of himself dead, was not a pleasant person to look upon.

If he had sprung up, old and wizened as he was; had let off a wild yell and had swung his fist at Jud, no matter what defeat and perhaps pain he might have suffered in a personal encounter with his bitter enemy, he would have arisen afterwards with his manhood intact. But he had not. He had failed himself, and never again after this night would Heber Caldwell be the same man. Jud looked away from him, turned his bitter stare upon the bullish man with the riot-gun, murmuring in a little voice:—

'Get out of here; tell Shaeffer and the others to stay out, too.'

The bodyguard did not move but his eyes dropped to the back of Caldwell's head. He was waiting. Jud, too, gazed upon Heber, waiting. Caldwell said: 'Go on, Sam.'

The bodyguard passed silently out of the office.

Jud backed off; stood loose in his joints with his weight carelessly distributed. 'Give me Buck Loring's hay option,' he murmured in the same small voice.

Old Heber bent forward rummaging a desk drawer. Without a word he passed over the paper. Jud stuffed it into a pocket never once looking away from Caldwell. 'Close the drawer,' he said, without knowing whether or not there was a pistol in it; not really caring for he knew Heber Caldwell had no spirit for using it if there was.

163

'Now Buck Loring's mortgage.'

This also was passed over by old Caldwell. Jud pocketed it with the first feelings of displeasure with himself beginning to stir within him. Hell; this was not like he'd imagined it would have been; this was no stormy triumph, no final last battle between titans, between uncompromising prairie pirates. This was taking from a cowed old man the hoarded treasures of his life. He stood a long moment in full silence gazing upon Caldwell. He was beginning to feel like a bully. A man, he thought now, with the weight of this knowledge coming down like a sledgehammer on his skull, was a better animal while he was striving and fighting, scheming and struggling, than he was when the need for fighting was past, when he stood upon his private pinnacle, triumphant.

'Call Shaeffer in here,' he said.

Caldwell touched a little bell upon his desk. Its insistent jangling sounded waspishly discordant over the deeper rumble of noises outside the door.

Luce Shaeffer appeared, a pale, thin young man whose eyes touched upon Jud Parker's great frame then fled to the slack face of his employer. Jud did not wait for Caldwell to speak.

He said: 'Keep the bank open until all those people have been paid off. Put up more lamps if you have to, and double the guard. But keep the

164

bank open.'

Shaeffer did not look again at Heber Caldwell. He said 'Yes, sir,' and backed out of the room, gently closed the door and faded out, lost to the attention, the thoughts, and the glances, of Jud Parker and Heber Caldwell.

'You're an old man,' said Jud evenly, forcing himself to a firmness of tone he did not feel. 'You've had Seward City in your pocket for a long time. You're a rich man, Caldwell. It's time you rested; took a trip maybe, so you can renew your perspective.'

A shallow breath, almost a sigh, passed Caldwell's grey lips. He still said nothing nor removed his eyes from Jud's face.

'You squeezed the guts out of these people. There was a time when that was the best way, but that's no longer true. Listen, Caldwell: Caleb Brownell's business is booming. By crowding him you've completely demoralised him. He's ready to burn his wagons and leave the country. What kind of sense does that make? Listen to me; you're in the banking business, Brownell's in the freighting business. You lend him money to expand, to grow, to make more money with—but you stay in your business and let him stay in his. This way you both prosper. If you'd busted him and had hired men to run his line you'd have had thieves and worse working for you; you wouldn't have had it all your way at all.

'You've got to take some time off, Caldwell; get your perspective back where it ought to be.'

Now Heber spoke: 'Yes; and while I'm taking this trip—what of my bank, my town?'

Jud again bent to lean upon the desk. 'Your son-in-law and I will run them, Caldwell. Like it or not we are now your pardners.'

Heber Caldwell's spirit was reviving. He said bitterly, 'You—you will never be any pardner of mine, Parker. I know your kind.'

Jud made a wintry smile, saying, 'You ought to, Caldwell. We were both struck from the same mould—but thirty years apart. You represent what used to be, I represent what now is—and Caldwell, young Bert Millam represents what is to be ten, fifteen years from now.'

Caldwell's pale eyes flickered with faint interest. 'You have it worked out,' he murmured. 'The dynasty continues doesn't it?'

Jud nodded. 'Perhaps for longer than you or I can see right now. Sharon will have sons.' Jud drew up off the desk, looked round for a chair, found one and kicked it up where he could sink down into it. 'In the East Vanderbilt created a dynasty; the Goulds did; the Rockefellers.' He bent an intent look upon old Heber. 'Out here, in this new land—why can't we do it? Generations of your blood growing with the West, Caldwell; does that sound so terrible to you?'

Old Heber's reviving spirit kindled visibly in

166

his cold stare imparting a warmth Jud had thought him incapable of. He said, 'No, frankly, it doesn't sound terrible to me, Parker. The trouble is I know your kind; you'll squeeze Sharon and Millam out. You'll own it all within a few years. Like you said—you're struck from the same mould I am.'

Jud shook his head at this. 'Caldwell, I told you—times have changed. No one man will ever again be able to have all the power and wealth. Look around you, man; this country is filling up, it's being settled and mined and farmed. Some day there'll be railroads out here. The future doesn't hold places for kings, it will be ruled by men working together. Get that through your skull, Caldwell.'

'I don't have much choice,' murmured the old man. Then he brightened perceptibly, saying to Jud with a look of hard interest in his face, 'How, exactly, did you do it, Parker? Sharon and Millam—the dynamiting of my bank—the riots—Brownell; how did you ever get it all to mesh like this?'

'By using people, Caldwell. By studying them, finding out their desires, their weaknesses, their hatred. Not by commanding them as you've always done.'

'That easy, eh?'

'That easy.'

Caldwell put a bony hand upon the desk, drummed with the fingers over an interval of thoughtful silence. Then he said, 'I'll pay you to leave the Dakotas, Parker.'

Jud made his low, hard smile, saying nothing to this.

Caldwell stopped drumming. He had made his feeble bid and it had been stonily rejected. He had not expected it to be accepted. He sighed, drawing closer to his desk.

'What are your terms, Parker?'

'One-third of the bank.'

'A third?' Caldwell's eyes widened.

'One-third to me, one-third to Mr. and Mrs. Millam. Cancellation of Buck Loring's mortgage, reinstatement of Mary Alice, my decision equally with yours in all matters pertaining to loans and how they're to be repaid.'

'Is that all?' asked the banker ironically.

Jud said, 'No; that's not all. All of it to be written into a legal contract by a Seward City lawyer and witnessed by your daughter, her husband, Luce Shaeffer, Buck Loring, Brownell and Mary Alice.'

'Any one else, Parker; sure you haven't forgotten someone?'

'Yes: You.'

'You're a pirate, Parker.'

'I guess it takes one to know one, Caldwell. You can refuse, you know.'

At this Heber Caldwell shook his head. 'I can't and you know it. Luce has kept me informed on how you've gone around getting folks' respect. If I refused you'd start this war all over again.'

'I would,' agreed Jud stoutly. 'Next time you wouldn't have any bank left at all.'

'You'd throw me to the mob, wouldn't you, Parker?'

'I would.'

Caldwell drew back a quavering breath and let it sigh past his lips. 'All right; you win. The terms are yours but I want to tell you one thing, Parker. I still hate your damned guts.'

Jud arose, passed over to the door, stuck his head through and bawled for Luce Shaeffer. 'Go get a lawyer,' he rumbled. 'Have him come over here at once.'

'Yes, sir,' responded Shaffer, and pranced away.

Jud turned back to bend a slow smile of bleak amusement upon Heber Caldwell. 'Go ahead and hate my guts,' he said quietly, eyes warming towards this old pirate. 'It's mutual, Caldwell. I don't trust you and you don't trust me. Damn you, Caldwell, I think we'll make a good team.'

Heber Caldwell laughed. It was a crackling, thin and ironic sound. Caldwell thought: 'By God I respect this man; I hate his guts but I respect him.'

CHAPTER EIGHTEEN

Jud did not leave the bank until the last customer had been paid off; he went with this grizzled miner to the front door and there halted, saying, with a hand resting easily upon the miner's shoulder: 'Be careful where you put that money, friend. After tonight there's going to be more than one throat cut.'

The miner considered his fist-grasped cash. He said uncomfortably, as though this new thought had been until that moment, entirely foreign to him, 'Damned if I don't think you're right, big feller.' He squinted upwards. 'You're Jud Parker, aren't you?'

'I am.'

'Well; folks set store by what you say. What do *you* recommend?'

Jud laughed. 'If it was me,' he said, 'I'd march right back in there and re-deposit that money. Caldwell's bank is as solid as a mountain.' He moved past. 'But it's your money, friend. Do as you like with it.'

He was making his way past little groups of people, placated now that they had their funds, and also exhausted by their hours-long excitement, when the grizzled miner turned about and re-entered the bank, the resolve upon his face an obvious thing.

170

This night there was a nearly-full moon. It rode overhead following big Jud Parker through Seward City as far as Mary Alice's house. He went forward towards the porch and out of dark shadows a white wraith rose up to meet him. It was Mary Alice. He turned towards her, saw her round, still face, saw the shape of her shoulders and the shining of her hair in that diffused pewter light. He remembered the great wave of warmth that had come from her lips surrounding him with its rushing sweetness.

She said: 'It's been a long night, Jud.'

He nodded, standing there letting the moments go past, saying nothing nor touching her; thinking that he had not, after all, got that white-painted house; thinking that in life so many things must be left undone, so many things were not on the surface as they initially appeared at first sighting.

'Sharon and Bert retired an hour ago, Jud.'

He ignored that. Her presence came strongly against him. He said, 'I won, Mary Alice. It's all down in writing; a third of the bank to me, a third to Sharon and Bert. You get your old job back. Loring's mortgage's torn up, his hay option too. My say to be equal with Heber's.'

He watched her face lift a little. She said simply, 'I'm glad for you. It's been hard, sitting here waiting; hearing that angry roar up in town.'

He reached forward to touch her. She didn't

171

move off from the pressure of his hands. He pulled her to him, swayed her body against him looking down into her face as it came up softened by starshine. He saw her mouth tremble a little, and when he bent low to meet her mouth with his lips it was like a great burst of heat, this meeting of their flesh. A rush of inexpressible things filled him inwardly. He stepped back.

'I know what it was like for you,' he murmured. 'Mary Alice—it may be like that again, some day.'

'I know, Jud. I thought of many things while sitting out here waiting. Once I said I didn't think life with you would be dull. It won't be; I think there will also be heartache and suffering too.'

'No,' he said against her hair while holding her. 'No, Mary Alice. I'll try; honestly I will.'

She burrowed against him. 'I don't want you to try, Jud. You couldn't change and trying to would only pain you, perhaps drive you away from me. You are what you are. I knew that the first night in the buggy. I accepted you that way—knowing.' She inched back to peer upwards. 'I don't believe I'd want you any different than you are, anyway. I'm no trembling girl; I know what life is like, Jud. It's struggle and fighting with little moments of happiness sandwiched in between. You're a man who lives for the fighting. I wouldn't want you any other way.'

He held her at arm's length admiring the fullness of her, the poise and great depth of calm. 'Damn,' he choked. 'A man could wander this world over time and again and not find another woman like you, Mary Alice. *My* kind of woman!'

'A pirate's wife?' she murmured, with rising inflection.

He threw back his big head and roared. Then he said to her, 'Old Heber called me that too; a pirate.'

'It fits, Jud. I don't think any description of you will ever fit you better.'

He was still grinning down at her, his eyes bright. 'And you; what are you if not a pirate's woman?'

She also smiled, but more tenderly, more gently. She did not speak but reached out with both hands to catch and hold his face in her cupped hands. 'And—perhaps some little pirates, later on?' she said softly to him.

'At least a dozen, Mary Alice.'

She led him to the edge of the porch where moonlight touched down its silvery substance upon the earth. There was not a sound coming from the town now; not a whisper nor even a sigh.

'It's after midnight,' she said without looking around at him. 'Aren't you tired? You look rumpled and older than you looked this morning.'

'I *am* older.'

He paused, facing fully for the first time a new thought which had been pecking at his consciousness since his first sighting of Heber Caldwell in Caldwell's office.

'Older and mellower,' he murmured. 'I want to tell you something, Mary Alice. It was a disappointment.'

She faced towards him.

'He didn't spring up and curse me; he didn't even let his bodyguard try to shoot me. He just sat there all shrunken and falling apart, staring at me like maybe he thought I'd reach over the desk and shake him like a rat.'

He lifted his eyes, let their gaze run out along the minutely-moving moonbeams and remain fixed in that soft-brilliant lustre far out.

'Some day that may also happen to me, Mary Alice.'

'Only if you let it happen, Jud. Only if you lose sight of everything that makes life worth living.'

He considered this for a time, then turned towards her saying quietly, 'You're right. You're dead right.' Then he continued to stare down at her, silent for another long while, before speaking again; saying: 'No, Mary Alice. It won't happen. Not with you beside me. You'll remind me if I get like that; you'll be there to keep me rational.'

174

'For as long as you want me,' she murmured. 'Or for as long as we're together, Jud.'

She felt for his hand, closed fingers around it, stood with him like that for what seemed to her to be a brief eternity when the world around them sang to her its solemn promise. Then she said: 'Jud, tomorrow is another day. Tomorrow you start building our future. You need rest.'

And she led him into the house, soft-dappling starshine touching down upon them until the door closed and they moved silently through darkness hand in hand, making no sound, closing out of their minds, each of them, the fire, the tumult, the danger, which had brought them to this peaceful moment.

Photoset, printed and bound in Great Britain by REDWOOD BURN LIMITED, Trowbridge, Wiltshire